**PURE
SLUSH
BOOKS**

summer

PURE SLUSH VOL. 12

First published August 2016

Stories copyright © Pure Slush and individual authors
Edited by Matt Potter

Pure Slush Books
4 Warburton Street
Magill SA 5072
Australia

Email: edpureslush@live.com.au
Website: http://pureslush.webs.com
Visit the Pure Slush Store: http://pureslush.webs.com/store.htm

Original cover painting *Until the Sidewinders Come Around* copyright © W. Jack Savage

ISBN: 978-1-925536-13-3

Also available as an eBook
ISBN: 978-1-925536-14-0

A note on differences in punctuation and spelling

Pure Slush proudly features (both online and in print) writers from all over the English-speaking world. Some speak and write English as their first language, while for others, it's their second or third or even fourth language. Naturally, across all versions of English, there are differences in punctuation and spelling, and even in meaning. These differences are reflected in the work *Pure Slush* publishes, and it accounts for any differences in punctuation, spelling and meaning found within these pages.

for

anyone

who ever longed

for winter to YES!!

finally be over

Snowflakes in the Middle of Summer
by Poor Louisiana

I've felt the coldest rain fall in the scorching heat

But I've been waiting all my life

For snowflakes to fall in the middle of summer

Fireflies shall dance for the first time

    without the night's approval

It is wise to believe in the impossible

Heat
by Penn Stewart

I showed up early, before the end of your shift, and saw you in the parking lot. You pushed your hair behind an ear. He said something funny and you laughed hard, your hand to your mouth, and stumble-stepped into a blush. He said something else, and you shook your head *no*.

But I've seen that *yes* before.

The smell of smoke hung in the summer air and the streetlights glowed with a halo of orange and gray. A fire truck screamed by on the road and you turned at the sound. Your eyes fell on me in my car. You stiffened and excused yourself. A tear of sweat wandered down my cheek and hung at the edge of my jaw.

Before you walked across the parking lot, before you opened the car door, before you got in, leaned over, and gave me a kiss on the cheek, and before we rode home in silence, I knew.

There was no breeze to cool the heat; the things that had bound us together loosened like frayed laces and slipped away.

Drinking Dream
by Laurie Kolp

I approach crowded pool bar
to order orange juice, lower visor
over bloodshot eyes.

An invisible man
with farmer's tan
and beer belly
nudges my elbow.

"How 'bout a screw-
driver, my treat."

Like all the other times,
I'd promised myself
not to drink before noon.
Vodka on tongue. One.

"Make it a double."

Loving It Hot and Sweaty
by Abha Iyengar

The Indian summer is always hot. This year it touches 50 degrees Celsius in a town in Rajasthan, and in Delhi, it's 42 degrees today and promises to become 44 degrees in a couple of days. Delhi was always hot in summer, famous for its hot dry wind, the loo. But now Delhi does not have a dry heat, the weather is humid too, so one sweats and sweats as one stands, the clothes sticking to the body. You may ask why I am making you feel hot under the collar on a similarly hot day where you live? Or you may want to be here with me in Delhi's heat, if an icy blizzard is raging outside your door.

Nonetheless, you are reading, so of course the Indian summer interests you. I write about the Delhi summer because perhaps I do not appreciate its worth, living as I have been in my city for a very long time. But if you are Russian, like a friend I have, you may have a totally different approach. Her name is Elena, and she is married to an Indian. She is lovely looking, but that is just something I am throwing your way to keep you interested. She goes shopping in Delhi for vegetables, very much like an Indian housewife. However, unlike the Indian housewife, Elena will go shopping in the midday heat of a summer afternoon for the above-mentioned vegetables. And sometimes for clothes, and sometimes just like that.

I met her one afternoon walking in Connaught Place. After the talk of maids, the price of food, how husbands, kids and the dogs, if we have them, drive us nuts, and all other such concerns are out of the way, we women, like Englishmen, will talk about the weather.

So after we had dispelled with the usual talk, I did mention the weather. The heat was coming out of my ears and hitting the dupatta wrapped around my face and neck. Sweat poured between my breasts and down my navel and slipped down my thighs. No, this is not intended as an erotic statement, but as the telling of an uncomfortable fact. My face was a hot red, furrowed with frowns. But Elena's face was calm. Her blond hair coiled in tendrils all over her exposed neck, her sleeveless, short cotton dress stuck to her slenderness.

I waved my hand in front of my face, and said, "Oh, this heat! I am dying to get home and drink five glasses of ice-dunked lemonade. And have the air-conditioning on full blast. And why are you out this time of the afternoon?" I mean, I was out on a needful errand, otherwise catch me saying hello to the outdoor heat.

She just smiled and said, "I want to be out in the sun. I love this heat." Mad dogs and Englishmen are known to go out in the rain. And some Russian women are known to step out in the Indian summer.

Summer
by Stephen V. Ramey

The slurp and grumble of rubber rolling over hot asphalt, a clattering grind as a hanger gives way and a section of rusted tailpipe drops down to taste the grayish grain. Laminar flow of sparks. It should put me in mind of the fireworks next week, the muffled boom and hiss, the intermittent squeals of color as the sky becomes a playground, movie screen, the only thing that matters. But it doesn't. I'm thinking of him, the old man down by the men's shelter earlier today.

"Nice ladder," he says. "I designed that ladder," he says. "Did you know?" And of course I don't, as his pale blue eyes water with expectation, as his hound-dog cheeks pull in with every rasping breath. He smells of body odor and something else. Fish guts? I don't know; it's not pleasant.

"You can do anything with that ladder," he says, and there's a hint of pride in his voice even as his trembling hand extends. I watch his palm, but it's only a handshake he wants, not money. There's a moment between us where neither of us is damaged and both of us are whole.

"I designed that ladder," he says, and I want to ask him when, where. I want to imagine him in a lab coat and goggles. Concentrating on something beyond another day.

I don't.

I don't imagine, don't ask, don't open myself to his attempted conversation. I'm afraid of the answers he will give, afraid of where interaction might lead. I think of the coins in my pocket, the credit cards in my wallet. I think that we'll both be dead in twenty years and none of it will matter.

"You can do anything with that ladder," he says.

You can do anything with anything, I think, *if you try*. I don't know if I believe it, but it's very American.

He frowns, blinks, swallows. I glance over my shoulder at the aluminum ladder leaning from my truck bed. It's one of those devices you can configure into multiple shapes depending on the job.

He's waiting for me. Sadness hangs between us, a gathering storm. I think of the cool that rain will bring, an honest cleansing, renewal. It's been so hot. And then I think of how different it must be to have to live in the elements, endure a downpour. How the sun can be a blessing too.

I force myself to meet his eyes and hold them. "It really is a clever design." My throat catches. I feel tears welling up behind my eyes, and I don't even know why.

"Thank you," he says, and his lips form a half-smile. "Have a blessed day."

I reach for my wallet, but he's already shuffling away. I watch him stop at a store window, gather himself, straighten his spine, arms reaching high and higher toward the impossible sky.

Meadow Girl
by Beate Sigriddaughter

It was summer. I sat by wild roses just in bloom. The ocean before me, delicious sun above, the fragrance of recently cut grass. Tiny white daisies that had bent to escape the mower already stood up again triumphant. Near me to the left were a mother with two children on a picnic blanket, a boy and a slightly bigger girl, both golden-haired in the sunlight, though the mother's hair was dark and fashionably cut chin-length and layered in back.

The girl hummed a song. Her braids were loosened by the breeze. She had picked a handful of daisies and held them out to her mother. "For you."

"Later," her mother said briskly, busy with packing up their picnic supplies.

Suddenly a skirmish, ending in a reprimand and an indignant defense.

"Mom, I was just sitting there. Tommy poked me with his picnic fork. Twice."

"Well, I didn't see it."

"Because your back was turned."

"Both times?"

"Yes, both times."

"Well, he's only five. He doesn't know what he is doing."

"He does so know."

The boy reached for his mother's hand. She took it. His eyes were round and blue and pleading.

"Mom, my arm hurts where he poked me."

"I don't want to hear about this anymore."

"You're listening to him."

"He hasn't said a word."

"He's holding your hand. That counts."

"And it tells me what a good little boy he is."

"But listen to me, too. Please, Mom."

"I've heard enough."

"No, you haven't."

"Of course I have."

There was one more thing the girl could do. The piercing scream. Even the roar of the water was not loud enough to drown it out.

"That's enough out of you, Missy. Come, Tommy. We'll go and leave her here until she is done screaming and being a bad girl."

Tommy shot his sister a proud look. Her screams swelled. She threw herself on the ground. Perhaps this had worked for her in the past. Today it didn't work. Today Tommy won.

Hand in hand, the mother and small son were already halfway up the meadow on the slope of the hill leading up to trees and houses on the right. They were almost to the top of the hill when the girl stood up, her face pink, her light blue dress darkened with grass stains. If they turned the corner onto the path among the trees, she would lose sight of them.

"Wait," she shouted and stumbled after them.

I picked up the small bunch of daisies she left behind.

Remembering
by Jessica Clements

Before our third date I went to your house to see you but you weren't there. "He's not here," your roommate said. She was a she and I couldn't remember if you'd told me this and wondered if it was a bad sign – not that she was a girl but that I couldn't remember. It was strange considering all the other things I had committed to memory, like the brown stain on the carpet outside the bedroom door of my fourth childhood home; the sound of my father's gum wrappers as he rolled them between his fingers; the squeak in the tin floor of your car.

Your roommate offered me a beer and then took one out for herself, popped the lid and drank.

"We're meant to be going out," I told her, and she nodded like she knew, pressing that cold beer against her skin.

I watched a droplet of water slide from the bottle and down the front of her top and I knew it was something I'd remember long after I'd forgotten the details of you. I'd remember in the way I remembered my father crinkling those gum papers long after he'd gone, and how my mother would grind her teeth when he did. Once, she'd left a bunch of gum in his top shirt pocket and watched them go round and round in the soapy machine. She pulled a straight face when my father held up his shirts all speckled with white dust, and claimed not to know what it was.

24

I thought about telling your roommate this, and about how it was her car that I imagined climbing into that day. But in the end I said nothing, just pictured that beer sweat still wet on her chest and glistening in the summer sun as we drove out onto the highway, thinking that in time I wouldn't be able to tell the difference between what had happened and had not.

Promising
by Matt Potter

"I know you're faking your Vitamin D count, Frances," I said, slipping off my sunglasses. "I can see it all over your face."

"It's low, but it's not as bad as everyone's saying it is," Frances said. "I'm not depriving my body of something it needs, Bridget." And she looked me straight in the eyes and her gaze was so direct and so honest and so *unblinking* I thought any second now, one of us is going to cry. "I'm not deliberately starving it."

"Then why aren't you out with us in the sun?" I asked. "In your bikini. Like we do every summer?"

And that was when – just as she lifted her arms to scratch her head – I saw the blotches on the underside of her arms, blue-black and sticky.

"My God!" I said. "Frances, look at your arms!"

And that was when I saw the inkwell on the table and the quill laying beside it and the pad of ink-splotched white paper laying beside that.

"I've got to do *something* this summer so I'm trying to be a poet," she said. "And I'm trying to make the words work on the page but I don't think I have any talent for getting this ink to work either."

"Why don't you use your computer?" I suggested.

She sighed. "I don't find the computer very inspiring."

"Then why don't you use my computer?"

She raised an eyebrow. "I mean computers in general."

"Oh." I slipped my sunglasses back on my nose and pushed them to the bridge. "Meanwhile, your Vitamin D is still bottoming out in the doldrums."

"*Look*," she said, "I'll swallow some capsules like everyone keeps *begging* me to and next week my Vitamin D count will be like I pretended it was." She picked up the quill and poised it above the paper. "I really wish people would stop worrying. It's just a silly old vitamin."

"Here's a thing: maybe you're more of a winter poet."

"You know I've always found summer more inspirational," she said. And then rolled her eyes.

I snatched my sunglasses off again. "Well, stranger things have happened, Frances! And isn't that one of the first things they teach you in poetry school, *truth is stranger than fiction*?!"

She dipped the quill in the inkwell.

"I may not know everything but I know a little about most things," I snapped.

"I never said you didn't know anything, Bridget." And then a headshake and she muttered, "There's just no pleasing you."

"It's not about *pleasing me*," I said, although, actually, really, it was. "Why don't you bring your paper and ink down to the beach?"

"Then I'll get sand on my poems."

"Then I'll blow the sand off," I said. And slapping my sunglasses back on my face, my arm sprang to a ringing salute. "Scout's honour."

"Hmmm," she said, "I don't know." And scratching the blue-black underside of her right arm with her left hand, she added, "I think your honour is about as promising as my poetry."

Spring Planting
by Judy Williams

Today, the grey squirrel dug up six strawberry plants,
four days after I'd placed them tenderly into composted soil,
leveling their crowns at just the right height above ground.
What was the point? Pulled up and scattered
with no sign of snacking.

Nearby, the brassicas huddle under row cover—
passive partners in my plot to thwart
the cabbage moth, dainty flutterer hell-bent
on having his way with the cauliflower, broccoli and kale.
No way.
I've set my sights on unblemished cole crops. He can take
his leaf-chewing caterpillars and leave my leaves alone.

In the potato bed not much is happening.
I peer anxiously downward each morning,
searching for green shoots, intent on avoiding
that green spud burn. So far, no one's showing her face.
Perhaps my wrinkled seed potatoes weren't such a bargain?
I bring only a naïve trust in luck to that cultivation.

Elsewhere, lettuce shines bright green, onions shoot
skyward, tomatoes are on steroids. French breakfast radishes
ram through soil. Beet greens and Swiss chard swagger,
while marigolds do double duty as beauty queens
and garden guardians. The peppers are popping,
peas entwining and kale standing erect. With the first blush
of summer's optimism, my garden has leapt out of the gate.
Ah summer! Bring it on!

Bondi
by Martin Jon Porter

The drinks boys' cries
are thwarted
by roaring waves.
Exploding whitewash
tumbles and crumbles
consuming ants
revelling
in a swishing puddle.

Infamous
territorial blue stingers
sequin the sand.
Lifesaver flags
are toothpicks on lemon slice.
Bellows through megaphones
only heeded
by gulling and gliding birds.

The breeze carries
romantic accents
of so many different origins.
Traced to bikini-ed brown bodies
and sleek flesh –
heat-drugged lizards,
lured.
While white pointers
constantly encircle,
torturing
married men.

Randomly propped clouds,
as if set for another TV show,
stain the infinite blue.
Apartments slope
jut-to-jut
parapets aplenty.

The 380
foregoes stops,
its frazzled driver
waving
apologetically.
Grand green carpet,
slanting to the beach,
cushions deserted commuters –
a place to sprawl
and wait.

Beach House Musing
by Lisa Stice

I want to live on the beach –
A house on a cliff
with stairs right down
to the sand
and waves.
I could sell necklaces on the side,
Beaded, handmade.
Hear myself say,
"This is my husband, Todd, the surfer.
He's a free spirit –
what I want to be."
But sand sticks to feet and legs.
Tracked into the house
and left all over the carpet
in little sandy piles
I would have to vacuum every day.

Falling Pieces of Skylab
by Michael Koenig

When I was a kid, I got hit in the head with a falling piece of Skylab. It had been in the news all summer, pieces of Skylab were falling; it could happen anywhere on earth. NASA engineers were trying to get it under control, but people were wearing construction helmets in the street and holding Skylab parties. As if any of that stuff could ever keep us alive.

It happened one day as I was walking home from school, a light thud on my head that almost knocked me over. When I looked down on the sidewalk I found this gnarled metal object roughly the size of a quarter that looked like it had been through a fire.

That looks like a piece of Skylab, a boy named Dennis Rasmussen said, a boy who often followed me home. *It almost totally burned up in the atmosphere.* He'd been reading about it obsessively, was convinced that we were all in danger, not just from heavy metal objects hurtling down from space, but also from the radiation. He'd started refusing to go outside for recess. Our teacher had taken to grabbing him by the shirt and dragging him out to the playground. We all thought it was funny.

I felt around on the top of my head to see if I was bleeding, took the debris home and showed it to my parents. Mom said it was interesting; Dad stared at his hours-old newspaper. I was keenly aware of how angry I usually made him. We pecked at each other like birds.

Let me look at your head, Mom said. *Do I need to take you to the doctor?*

I'm fine!

I adjourned to my room to scribble out my homework, put the debris in an ashtray I'd stolen from Marlotti's and started writing my letter to NASA, consulting my little piece of space junk for inspiration. Maybe they'd offer a settlement. I wouldn't even have to sue.

My mom threw away my falling piece of Skylab a couple of days later, in the course of one of her periodic magazine inspections. I dug through the wet food and Kleenex, but it was gone. I sent NASA my letter anyway, and a couple of months later I got a letter back, thanking me for my interest in the space program. By then, the rest of Skylab had come crashing down somewhere in Australia and Dennis Rasmussen had started reading a book called **Limbo of the Lost,** about all the ships and airplanes lost in the Bermuda Triangle. My head wound had scabbed over and was nearly healed.

I put one of the NASA stickers they sent me on my notebook. I wanted to be a scientist now, along with a few other things. I'd sit there in class, fingers tracing the unknown geography on the top of my head, searching for the last remaining traces of my bump from falling pieces of Skylab.

Aptitude
by Linda Ferguson

You could say I don't like my job. I hear my boss at night. He reminds me to dress neatly, to sit up straight and smile when clients come in, to pick up my typing speed because he needs his reports A.S.A.P. His words tap across my skull as I twist in the hot sheets. It's not just his voice, though – I see him too. So clearly. The smooth golf tan, the silver side-burns, the gold pen poised between his clean fingers.

Last year I was a computer programmer, a job I'd landed just three weeks after graduation. I had an office with a window and a view of the park, and I ate lunch with the other programmers. When the company went bankrupt I was sure I'd have another job within a month or two. Maybe it would even be closer to home, with a nicer lunchroom.

Weeks slipped by. I had interview after interview. I shook hands and smiled, showed samples of my work. Every Friday I sent the unemployment office the names of the companies I'd contacted – proof that I was out there pounding the pavement, not just curling up on the couch and licking the salt off potato chips.

This job was listed as "Marketing Coordinator: Write proposals for small engineering firm. Some office work." The unemployment counselor insisted it was ideal for someone with my technical skills. I'd been out of a job for eight months. I had bills that were overdue. My little sister, who sold closet organizers on commission, kept asking, "What do you do all day?" My mother referred to me as "the lady of leisure." I felt like the same skinny geek I'd been in middle school P.E. – the one who couldn't throw a basketball within five feet of the backboard. I put on a skirt and a pair of heels and hand-delivered my application to the engineering firm.

On my first day, Jerome C. Hawthorne himself showed me to my desk – up front, complete with a headset and a 10-line telephone. He said this arrangement was temporary. I'd get my own cubicle and start writing marketing proposals when their girl Clara came back from maternity leave. The phone rang. He motioned to it, graciously. I put on the headset. The call was for someone named Tom. I heard a sing-song voice over the speaker paging him. It took me a minute to realize that was me, sounding so sweet. Down the hall, someone snickered.

My new boss stood over me. I wanted to ram the phone down his throat, but I remembered my student loans. Line two was blinking. I pressed the red button and said, "Good morning, Hawthorne & Associates," just as smooth as you please. Jerome C. beamed.

That was last June. It's July now, and there's no word of Clara's return. Jerome C. recently called me into his office for a performance review. He said I was showing genuine aptitude.

Man on a Wire
by Paul B. Cohen

I was fresh in the neighborhood. At the boarding house, I'd met Mrs. Bedford, the landlady. She had a definite mustache, and monstrous arms, and I confess I was intimidated. Her manner, though, was cordial, but I didn't want to spend too long in her company. I needed to get out, I needed to find a job, but that could wait until Monday. It was a glorious Saturday afternoon, and I wanted to meet people.

After I had unpacked my valise, and lined up my books on the oak shelves above the fireplace, I went for a walk. The thoroughfare was busy without being oppressive, and I was glad to have arrived in a new city with all it could offer.

I looked up. Twenty feet above my head, etched against the azure summer sky, was a man on a wire. How could this be? Yet it was so: a man was inching along a cable running from Eastman to Fairmont Street.

Holding a pole for balance, he wore a bowler and flared trousers, like Charlie Chaplin. Several automobiles passed underneath, indifferent to the aerial show.

But what if he fell? I was only partially reassured by the supple grace of his delicate, careful movements. What if he plummeted onto the cars below?

He did not fall. Instead, he edged past a couple of suburban homes, until he was lost from sight behind a line of trees. I ran across the road; I had to meet this adventurer.

Intrusively, I let myself through a gate and veered to the left of a two-story house. A stepladder leaned against a sycamore. On the lawn, the high-wire artist was calmly setting down his apparatus.

"Sir, how on earth did you do that?" I asked. My breath was shallow. "How d'you keep your balance?"

He turned to me, and removed his bowler, liberating glorious chestnut hair. And I saw that the lipstick worn was cerise.

I asked, "What's your name?"

"Women can be acrobats, you know," the man on the wire said.

Of course, he was no longer on the wire. He was no longer he. And, it seemed to me, I was no longer alone.

Bare Feet
by Cynthia Hoffman

Culver City 1955

In the summer I never wore shoes. Toes freed of socks, sandals or even flip flops.

The hot sidewalk in summer slipped up my legs warming, finally, my winter-free soles.

On hot, hot days, I ran through the sprinklers on giggly tip-toes over the prickly mowed grass.

On Sundays, once or twice a month when my father had a day off, my parents packed a cooler full of fruit, sandwiches, and a thermos of coffee, and stuffed the beach umbrella, old towels and thin blankets into the trunk for the long ride to the beach. I rode in the back with my head out the window. I could smell the ocean in the rushing air long before we arrived.

After fussing with bundles across the hot sand, the broad beach umbrella, green with faded orange strips, was planted in the sand like so many others – a sea of umbrellas up and down the shore.

I didn't swim but I did run to the water's edge, wading in just close enough for the tide to froth around my ankles, leaving my footprints and tiny air holes of clams and crabs in the wet sand as the water receded.

Careful to map my course from *our* umbrella, I checked and rechecked behind my shoulder lest I got lost.

Returning to my parents for the obligatory plum or sticky peach – "eat something!" – I cajoled and begged for fifteen cents to buy a snow cone.

The white wooden food and beverage stand was far away from the shore near the parking lot. Walking on burning, hot sand in bare feet was a dangerous art. I would take a beach towel, throw it on the sand in front of me, run to the end of it, hop on one bare foot and throw it down again. Sometimes I'd sneak a foot on the corner of someone else's towel, corner hopping from one to the other.

Standing in line on broiling asphalt, hopping from one foot to the other, my prize of a glistening, cold snow cone with red cherry and green lime syrup was worth it. Finding shade on a bench under one of the round kiosks, I concentrated on the taste sucked through the little red straw, and full-on bites of crushed ice.

I returned to my parents under the shade of our umbrella, again, mapping my course over my shoulder, counting, my face and hands sticky with wonderful, sweet syrup.

How embarrassing it was to be wrapped in a threadbare towel by my mother, stripped of my bathing suit, and wiped down like some baby. There will be no sand in the house!

Dressed in a sun suit, the bottom of my feet black with tar that my mother scrubbed clean before a foot was set in the gray Kaiser for the long ride home.

I would lay on the back seat watching the trees and telephone poles fly by the windows before falling asleep.

Memories of an Unknown Summer
by Kristina England

My mother's hands are scalded, too much washing of dishes. Her veins pulse through like a million little heart beats.

It is July and it's not yet hot enough to make my skin stick to the kitchen chair. I am twenty-one, the age where we are half between adult and child.

My mother runs the sink to muffle my father's cries.

"I'm dying," he moans from down the hall. "Why would you do this to me, God?"

Once a tarot reader, he has a hard time accepting the unknown. Where is the Hang Man, why will he not flip over and show his shameful face?

My father is shriveling, has lost fifty pounds, and the doctors can't tell us what's wrong. The word colitis is batted around like a fly we can't kill.

I look at the car keys. They seem to say, "Take me," as if I was in my own Wonderland.

I turn to my mother. "Let's go to the movies."

"I can't leave him here... by himself."

"He's not going anywhere," I say as if I could read the future.

Her eyes shift back and forth from the sink where the dishes don't need any more rinsing, to my father's voice, then back to her own legs, as if assessing their ability to run.

She has always been a strong-shouldered woman. Her body tenses. She walks down the hall and says, "We're going to a movie."

My father starts crying. I can hear the wetness in his voice. It will rain this week or at least that's what the weather men say and they are the worst kind of predictors.

My mother is standing at the kitchen doorway. She has her purse in hand. We descend the stairs, away from the storm, the lightning that keeps striking our hearts.

We go to the theater where it is cool, fill our bodies with over-buttered popcorn.

The wheel of fortune keeps spinning. We take a two-hour break from holding our breath, from waiting to see where it will land.

Summer Love
by Guilie Castillo Oriard

Even the spiky leaves of the aloe plants are turning a bluish brown. The heat has baked the yard into fine, fine dust, and steamed all the blue out of the sky. The longest days of the year blur into a blistering glare so dense it flattens anything that breathes, anything with the minutest will to exist.

Except Mama.

Incomprehensibly untouched by the riot of heat, my diffident, melancholy mother has chosen this merciless summer to find happiness. She radiates it like a fucking furnace, and everything else—our quiet routines, our painstaking truces, our slow existence *à deux*—melts in its presence.

"He's a dream." She stretches out next to me on the veranda. The Portuguese tiles beneath us retain only a trace of the night's cooler temperatures.

"I'm happy for you, Mama."

She smiles like she can't hear the sarcasm and leans over to kiss my forehead. "This is the real thing, baby. I can feel it."

"You seeing him again tonight?"

"Just dinner after work. I'll be home by nine."

Her footsteps crunch halfway down the gravel path, then stop. "What are you doing today?"

She's standing half in sunlight, half in the shade of the old *kenepa* tree. She can't suspect; her cup-runneth-over state keeps her insulated.

I hold up the textbook. "Study. SATs are in October."

She shakes her head, hands on hips, a movie smile of pride on her lips. "My baby, off to college at sixteen."

I smile back, but the effort is wasted; she's already turned the corner. A jangle of keys, a squawk of metal from the car door, the roar of the engine, and she's gone. The same breeze that soothes the air she left so inflamed with her high hopes washes away the whiff of exhaust in her wake, too.

He calls me things he probably uses with Mama too, and some I know he doesn't, if for no other reason that what I bring to him—things that shove his fear and his principles under the shag carpet of lust and out of the way—those things my poor Mama, bent at the knee in gratitude for his attention, can never give.

In the mirror, the golden skin of my breasts glows with the light of late afternoon as I pull the t-shirt on. He's watching from the bed, my cigarette between his fingers, so I make it slow, this strip-tease in reverse, and watch the bedsheet twitch at his groin. *A + for stamina, Geezer.*

He looks away, though, and I sigh. Here it comes. His weekly *This has to stop* crisis-of-conscience bullshit (he knows I know it's bullshit).

Instead he says, "Why haven't you told her?"

Which throws me only for a moment. "Why haven't you?"

He finds my gaze in the mirror, holds it. "I love her."

I love her, too.

Letter to N: This Summer
by Edward Reilly

The stink of burning grass after rainfall, galahs wheeling
Through treetops along the grey river, skies overcast:
Perhaps it will rain enough to put an end to the bushfires
Even though there is talk of another heat spell next week.
The tomatoes are doing well, plenty of the small *romanos*,
But the *grosse lisse* are fruitless, just as are our neighbour's:
Maybe a bad batch, even the local newspapers commented.
Since then, advertisements have appeared for
        organic seedlings.
I suppose they imply the plants have been raised from seed,
Watered with virgins' tears at midnight on a full Moon,
Manured by buried cows' horns, the usual vatic nonsense,
But if they yield halfway decent fruit, then why snipe?
As you may have seen on the BBC, our coast is on fire,
From the Cape to Lorne people have fled to the beaches,
Wading into the strangely slick waters to escape the flames
Sweeping down from the hills' crowns roaring
        like a banshee,
Flinging embers out and over their heads, waves turning red
And even the fish fleeing into deeper waters. I remember
What it was like in 1983 when we took flight from Lorne,
Trying to get past Anglesea before they closed the exits.
We made it. Children sobbing and dog whining in the back,
Radio crackling with drift and static so badly I turned it off,

Besides, those blokes in the Big Smoke weren't witnesses
To what we had seen, and felt: all hysteria and
        pointless noise,
Then the smooth platitudes from those who weren't here.
At least you gave us a hot meal and a place to stay the night,
And didn't rattle on about unprovable theories of
        climate change,
Like the endless parade of faces on the flickering screen.
Strange how the images were bent and warped by smoke.
You said something about the new digital service to come
When this sort of thing wouldn't happen, new technology
Promises us a better, some say an even more fulfilling life,
But the signal still does disintegrate into baffling squares
So that we see ghosts shifting across a shimmering screen
On a still summer night when Neptune sports with
        our Science
Or the Moon shines too brightly in late summer nights.
They suspect arson, or it could have been a faulty powerline.
In either case the boys will need to wait until it's quite safe
To drive into the ranges and look around the fire's seat.
Surely no one would have been crazy enough to
        have been up there!
When the cool change and rain came in, before sunrise,
A chorus of birds went into full-throated, lusty singing,
Rousing me out of bed to make myself a coffee and toast
Whilst the rest were still sound asleep. What a noise!
Honeyeaters trilled, mynas scurried around garden beds,
Magpies carolled their territorial anthems, ravens cawed.
A neighbour's dog remonstrated against the incoming wind,
And a blanket, still draped over the clothes line, flapped.
Thanks for the phone call, as I said we're in no danger,
And we'll stay on for the coming month, maybe longer.

Day Nine of a Road Trip
I Wasn't Expecting
by Alicja Zapalska

(i)
The day rivers away, silver across the horizon.
We drive a mile before stopping, landing
on a road in wait of ourselves. You watch the ground
for fear of it leaving. The horizon holds empty.
Instead
I tell you stories: a mouth opening to an ocean.
A man in love travelling the world
with a hole in his heart.

(ii)
The road tugs upward and we kiss each hill.
Words shrink at night and I practice fitting them
into my mouth, in the space between
the dashboard and steering wheel.
How is this not beautiful, the apology
unfolded stammer, threaded voice across each word?

(iii)
Lightning presses a hesitant touch to the ground.
We sit encased in glass and I ask you to trace
each eyelid with the same precision,
the same trembling fear.

Pool Shark
by Steve Carter

sleek boy
black hair
back from the water
throws a bright coin
just missing two girls
unnoticed
in the water

runs, leaps
sleek dive
into the pool
to the water's depth

comes up with it
in long fingers
breaking the surface
shining

Running
by Jenny Lapekas

My father runs through the same snowflakes that cover my mother's window boxes. They batter his face like frozen needles as he jogs uphill, downhill, past the house where he used to live. His skin is weathered from his days as a lifeguard, as a boyfriend who sings in cars and dances on beaches.

He lags down our long driveway, hands on hips, eyes fixed like the buttons on the Benetton coat he brought me from London last year. His wheat brown head hides beneath a ski cap, and his face is flushed but sober. His ears are wrinkled orange peels, waning fruit that sit behind his eyes.

Inside, he leans beside the sink and guzzles ice water, words trapped in a narrow throat. His mouth, pressed in ice, melts and simmers every so often. When he does speak, I feel like a thief, smuggling the words with tight fists and sharp jaw. When it's not glistening with the work of running, his face looks like my own.

He loops his finger in a flat pocket brush and smoothes it over his hair in several even strokes, never looking in a mirror. While he follows flight plans in the sky, my father's crippled sense of direction pushes him to shovel sidewalks and wipe messes clean, migrating as each season dictates.

He searches for his work boots, necessary even for car rides to get ice cream in November. He pauses and stands before the window to gaze across the cornfield, like a tragic statue, his hands clasped together behind his back. He sees himself down the lane, staining things with wine and distracting his original family with lame props, like Christmas parties and summers on the island.

His TWA wings sit on a slate countertop, laid down and replaced with a glass of whiskey the night before last. Peeling wallpaper exposes the bright daisies that grew on these walls before we arrived. It catches the brief sunlight of short days, holding its shadows until winter yawns into a warmer creature.

"Where are we going, Dad?"

"Let's play it by ear," he says as he changes his shoes.

Diving Through
the Golden Arches
by S. L. Kerns

When I was a kid growing up in the backwoods of Kentucky, I couldn't wait for the winter snow to melt and the sun to give me the inevitable first-days-of-summer sunburn. It was with the crack of a baseball bat that I knew, we all knew, spring was here and summer was near.

None of my best buds were on the ACHS varsity team, but as soon as the heat warmed the waters, we'd all meet up at the cliffs. My friends were athletic but non-conforming individuals with wild hairstyles, and unfashionable clothes. At the cliffs, clothes didn't matter, because we often didn't wear any in that secluded area, just a twenty-minute hike through the woods and away from the main roads of that sleepy town.

"Cannonball," shouted my tallest friend, his blond mohawk flapping in the breeze while he ran towards the fifty-foot drop and jumped. He bombed the still water with a colossal splash. The rest of the gang followed suit, like an airstrike on the bass below. If my friends asked me to jump off a bridge, I guess there was proof I would.

All summer, they'd head to the cliffs, but usually on Saturdays, when I was often stuck working at McDs.

My managers were McBlob, and McBitch—nicknames they had earned from the crew. I hated joining the elderly breakfast crew at five a.m. on the weekends; it was earlier than I had to wake up for school the rest of the week.

One Saturday morning with the lobby and drive-thru lines backed up, McBitch and McBlob running around barking orders, I received a telephone call.

"For you," McBitch said, carelessly dropping the yellow telephone in my hand, the spiral cord pulling me away from my duties. "Make it snappy."

I pressed my ear to the receiver. "Dude, we are going cliff diving. You comin'?" It was my mohawked friend.

"Man, you called me on the *work* phone. How the hell can I? You know I can't go."

"It's McDs! Just quit."

"You make it sound so easy."

"Because it is. When you look back on life, what are you going to remember, working at McDs, or swimming with your friends?"

He had a point. I hung up the phone, threw off my apron, and strode out to the joys of friendship and summer, leaving the golden arches behind me for good.

Changing Seasons
by Brad Garber

The squalls move through this time of year like wild children dashing across the yard squealing for inexplicable reasons pushed along by a very large hand and indoor plants strain against the windows like bears awaking from a long fat sleep and against the wall sits an untuned guitar missing one string there is rust on the knife and the Adirondack chairs are stacked along the railing the time for movement drawing near like when the plate is garnished the steak seared the beans still crisp and the entrée is about to be served all in deft and choreographed dance and I wait with knotted gut and leaking mouth my tongue tasting the ground for danger or a nice flat rock while glaciers continue to pull their fingers back in mock horror and the sea reclaims its own but olive oil continues to be my choice of sunscreen the death of vegetables seeping into my skin and construction crews scrape mastodon tusks out of Seattle mud feathered bone rocks are sold in China to tourists and curled shells of death adorn display cases of jewelry stores while this tiny globe thing contracts squeezing its innards out across wheat fields like angry bees armies of ants and societies of sewer rats all plotting to take over where we left off our breasts pulled into the spring skies with summer coming on to remind us of the demise of "Sol" in unpredictable time a last searing moment when all will be stopped in its tracklessness strewn into the dark matter again to coalesce into hearts and lungs the loci of understanding and fear like that is how matter is destined to be a nervous system with energy nodes waiting to be destroyed again and again and again so I will throw the door open and sweep accumulations out into the maw of the cycle riding the updraft into another anxious season my arms like one more set of wings.

Last Summer
by Alex Reece Abbott

People expect sand, surf and sun-bronzed bodies when they hear about summer in California.

But often the foghorn lows and her mournful cry carries across the Pacific strait. Heaven reaches down to hug earth and bay, and fog haunts that famous vermilion span, damp tendrils clinging.

No Castro clone, in a sea of chinos, denim and polo shirts, he was quintessentially English; clipped accent, tortoiseshell glasses, tweedy jacket and polished Oxfords. Never prissy, always precise. The guy who had it all together.

Smart and funny, with boyish charm he nailed a faltering sponsorship deal for a film festival in less than an hour. Facing a tide of financial threats and funders with attitude, outwardly things ran like clockwork, all safe in his hands. People expected him to glide from success to success. Only his crinkled, dark hair wouldn't quite bend to his will, despite the wax.

His suits murmured: *Savile Row, take me seriously.* Did he plan that last outfit? The report said white jeans with a red and green flannel shirt. Strangely festive. Were his pockets heavy with stones, like Virginia?

Naturally, for his final show of shows the planner chose one of the world's top engineering achievements: oh so cinematic Golden Gate Bridge. Not red, but International Orange; pedant detail he'd have relished.

Olympic divers do not jump, they fall in elegant descent. They do not plummet. They do not drown. Did he face those two hundred feet without hesitation, like the circus man on the grainy newsreel, who dives into the swimming pool from the top of the water tower, again and again?

Did he swoop like a swallow, or fall like a rock? Pulled by velocity and gravity, did he somersault? Was there a second, a moment when he wanted to turn around? Or, did he embrace the cold Pacific, as she swept him south in her seven knot grip?

Only thirty have survived that fall. One said that the instant his feet left the steel plate, regret hit him. But those closest to the Englishman with the name of a bird said that he'd achieved the closure he'd craved. Yet, to have one last conversation. To understand what was going on beneath his wayward quiff that night, before that rainy morning when he took the pedestrian walkway. Before he left his hand-stitched, leather satchel against the mid-span railing, before he made one last flight from thirty-three years of turmoil.

Seventy-six summers after it was first recommended, the new safety net will catch others. Too late for him, or the sixteen hundred who've already fallen – twenty-five every year.

But, would he have wanted to be caught beneath the bridge in those steel wires? Those who knew him best expect that he'd have found another day, another place to leave this earth.

At the baking beach today, see an osprey, how she hovers, totally in control, before descending gracefully to the glittering, briny sea. And, think again of the man who had it all together.

Middle Earth Café: Nakusp, B.C.
by Kersten Christianson

It's a muggy summer day here
wood trim like dark ale
contrasts with perky raspberry-hued
carnations in pottery vases on each table.

Blank note cards in altered boxes, photographed
and bejeweled, sit out on the counter,
Mandala Moon Divine Arts.
The magic of the Kootenay.

A postcard stamped *New Zealand* boasts
Frodo and Sam-wise in capes and smiles.
Altars of wood and stone appear
in random corners of the café.
Stained glass moons and World Tree
adorn the windows, along with a sign,
a reminder to be kind:

Don't piss off the fairies.

The End of Everything
by Edward O'Dwyer

The woman in the café
tells me it's the end of everything,
not in those exact words, though,
as she pours my coffee,
late-May sunshine filtering cloudily
into the room,
lighting up the quiet beauty
of her (I'm guessing) Polish face.
As I turn to choose a table
I hear her add,
a kind of afterthought,
maybe not even to me,
rather a word of resignation
in her own ear,
that, as well, it's the beginning of nothing,
although, again, not in those exact words.

Fruits of Summer
by Iris N. Schwartz

Grape tomato in my mouth,

thin-skinned smoothness under tip of tongue,

triggers a time

when my first love asked me to read

The Sensuous Man and *The Sensuous Woman*,

to perform lingual exercises with a sweet white grape,

the better to appreciate

all we would experience

in his lushly carpeted room,

on his sturdy mattress,

the family dog

wagging his tail as he watched.

Infernal Cravings
by J. J. Steinfeld

Yesterday, on the hottest day of the summer, a record-breaking temperature, in fact, my next-door neighbour, an unsmiling man with a huge barking dog that has been disrupting my otherwise quiet evenings for close to two years now, went to the corner store to purchase cigarettes and candy bars, I'm fairly certain, for he seems to have had an addiction to both judging by what I saw evening after evening when he sat on his patio smoking and consuming candy bars in large quantities, his poor excuse for a canine voicing its high-decibel displeasure with existence, and that next-door neighbour went to Hell instead, quite the re-routing. He was known to mock the Eternal as he smoked and devoured his candy bars, and I understand from good authority, that is, a world-renowned theologian from down the street, my former next-door neighbour is now standing in an endless line, waiting to make his purchase, the heat exceeding even yesterday's record-breaking summer temperature. Reader of this sad little tale, if you have a craving for cigarettes or candy bars, think twice before walking out the door in the summer heat.

In the summerblaze
of a smooth night
by R. Bremner

In the summerblaze of a smooth night

a Ray Charles path calls out and

our shadows cross the billabongs

to drink a spotted wine

while your brilliance burns my

flammable brain and we seek

the stars and scars of a reading

at our favorite venue where

we sweat in the summerblaze

of a smooth and spectacular

night and a hot July rain feels

so good.

1967

by Len Kuntz

It was the Summer of Love, but not where we lived.

Gordy's dad had a new girl who didn't care what Gordy's dad did, and so the beatings continued.

"I'm going to kill him," Gordy said.

The acne on his face was as bad as ever, ripe and raw, the sun making it worse when it should have made it better. What made him wince, though, were the fresh stripes and bruises under his shirt, across his back.

"You're not going to kill anyone," I said, though I wasn't completely sure. "Besides you're only thirteen."

We sat on cracked pavement in the back of a liquor store by a dumpster that smelled like rotting carcasses. Gordy wanted to get drunk again, so we were looking for an adult who might help us.

"What's age got to do with anything?" Gordy asked. "In my mind, I've already killed him plenty of times."

"Thinking is different than doing."

"That's exactly what I'm talking about."

Summer should have been the best time for a kid, but it was Gordy's worst season. As much as he hated school, it was a safe haven that ate up hours.

We watched a butterscotch Pontiac pull into the lot, coughing black exhaust.

"That guy'll do it," Gordy said, wincing again as he stood.

The guy had gray hair, was tall and thin but with a huge gut. We caught him a few yards before going in.

"Hey man, think you could do us a kind one and get a bottle of Jim Beam? It's an extra five for you," Gordy said.

The guy looked neither surprised nor annoyed. "You want me to break the law?"

"What's the law all about anyway?" Gordy said. "It's just something somebody made up."

"Do I look like a criminal?"

"You look nice enough, I guess."

"I am *nice enough*," the guy said, grinning now.

"Hey, I'm not going to suck your dick or anything. I'm not that desperate."

The guy stopped smiling, held out his hand and Gordy passed him the wadded up bills.

When he came out, the guy thrust a sack at Gordy.

"Thanks, man," Gordy said. "Say, you know if you could maybe get me a gun?"

The guy's eyes flung open as if blasted by a gust of air. "Get the hell away from me."

"I was just asking."

We watched the Pontiac fly off, took our same spots back by the dumpster where scratching noises came from inside.

Gordy took a long pull of whiskey, then I did.

"It's gonna have to be a knife, a rope or wire," Gordy said.

"Stop with that shit."

"It's me or him."

Inside the dumpster something squealed and scurried.

Gordy took another long pull. He was the only friend I had.

I closed my eyes and lifted my face to the sun. I saw our futures, Gordy's and mine. I pictured a funeral without either of us there.

"Okay," I said, "I'll help you."

"With what?"

"What needs getting done."

Walking a Goat
by MK Punky

Walking a goat
Strolling a sweater
Redacting a ruminant originally meant for meat
This incomplete canine lacks incisors
and emotional attachments to
    All that must one cold day die
The bluebells
    The daffodils
        Garlic mustard sprouts
        Signaling summer
Beneath cloven hooves

Amiable impostor heavy with rain
Mobile reservoir irrigator
Obliterator of reputations
Chaperone of forest perambulations

How did you know I need a friend

Summer Stock
by Jan Chronister

Costumes hang in dark theatre
waiting to bloom on stage.
Exotic perennials of purple velvet
blue brocade
flowering for
a few brief weeks
glowing in spotlights
adorning, adored
then packed up and stored
for next summer.

Gun Wounds Again?
by Michael Coolen

During the summer of 1974 I was a Peace Corps Volunteer in the Republic of the Gambia, West Africa. To escape the evening heat, I often walked down to the local air-conditioned cinema, about a fifteen-minute stroll from my hut. The outside walls of the cinema had two rows of posters showing the coming attractions. The top row posters advertised Bollywood films, while the bottom row advertised Kung Fu films.

In particular, I remember one poster advertising a film titled *Stranger from Canton*, whose plot stated that there was only one martial-arts expert in the world who could possibly "defeat the pig-tailed Manchurian villain who uses the braid of his hair as a lethal weapon of total destruction."

Although the summary really broke me up, the real laughs came when I read the English subtitles during the film. I'm not sure my mumbled responses amused the theater-goers around me.

—*Gun wounds again?* —So true. Gun wounds can be really annoying.

—*I am damn unsatisfied to be killed in this way* —As compared to?

—*The bullets inside are very hot. Why do I feel so cold?* —Air circulating through the bullet holes?

—*I got knife scars more than the number of your leg's hair!* —I'm not sure how many knife scars were involved because the Chinese fighters weren't very hairy.

Then there were those subtitles that really made no sense at all.

—*How can you use my intestines as a gift?* —Is your girlfriend a zombie?

—*A normal person wouldn't steal pituitaries* —Duh. They can't be used as transplants.

—*You always use violence. I should've ordered glutinous rice chicken.* —Adopting a gluten-free diet might help reduce your tendency to be violent.

—*I threat you! I challenge you meet me on the roof tonight for a duet!* —As a singer, I think this subtitle demonstrates how civilized musicians can be when handling conflict.

Then there are those subtitles that seem to be the result of mistakes by an early version of Siri taking dictation:

—*This will be of fine service for you, you bag of the scum. I am sure you will not mind that I remove your manhoods and leave them out on the dessert flour for your aunts to eat."* —None of my aunts would ever have treated me that way.

—*Yah-hah, evil spider woman! I have captured you by the short rabbits and can now deliver you violently to your gynecologist for a thorough extermination.* —Umm?

—*Now I feel flatulent, and you did it.* —I've often said that to a plate of refried beans.

—*I please your uterus. You kiss my toes. It's fair.* —This seems fair to me, too.

That scorching summer of 1974 also sent me to the cinema at night to watch a variety of Bollywood films, whose trailers were longer than some non-Bollywood films. Tedious, but worth the air conditioning.

There's a Croc in Your Backyard
by Walter Giersbach

Morty called while I was drinking my coffee and pulling the burning toast out of the thing at the same time. The call made me drop my cup. "What!" Afraid I wasn't too Christian answering my neighbor, but the summertime temperature was going up to 105 again today.

"Just want to alert you. There's a crocodile in your backyard."

"Are you out of your damn mind?" I slammed down the receiver and looked for a paper towel to clean the mess. Thing is I'd heard the warnings. "Crocodiles everywhere," the TV news reader said like it was a joke. Not funny. I knew those monsters were out there because one ate my Jack Russell terrier last week. It wasn't much of a dog but there's such things as property rights, even with the Democrats in the White House and liberals taking away what little I got.

Thing you got to watch about the Dems is that they want to help you cross the street, then they won't let go when you get to the other side. That's what I always explained to my wife Hildy, but she's dead now so that's not a good example. Anyway, that's what I told one of those socialist bell-ringers after my Jack Russell got digested, "Don't ever be knocking on the door of my trailer again!" I really got in her face. That'll make an impression on her college-girl mind when she goes back to her Commie brainwash factory.

I turned up the air conditioning and found a couple shells for my shotgun. Just in time, too, cause there was an awful racket down by the dumpster where we toss our garbage. The dumpster's next to a big blue box where the left-wingers want us to throw our tin cans, as though that's gonna get me a job.

I ran out with my 12-gauge and saw this overgrown piece of luggage chomping on somebody's animal. Hard to tell what kind of animal, but it was small enough to be a pain in the ass. Good riddance. And I shot the walking suitcase. Another good riddance.

Then I called Morty back. "That weren't no crocodile I just shot by the dumpster. It was an alligator. Can't you get your facts straight, you old fart?"

Well, the day was hot as hell so I turned on the TV and opened a beer. Maybe one of those politicians might come up with the answers I'm still waiting for. I don't recollect being menaced by gators when Bush and Cheney were in the White House and Hildy was alive, but maybe I was too optimistic that the future was still in front of us.

Hildy would've told me to put some charity in my heart. But, as bad luck would have it, Hildy passed away from a heart attack. Now, I've got to stick around, recycle tin cans, and fight gators invading our community. Doc told me last week he thinks I may have the cancer too.

I got a little inkling that someday there won't be no more gators to fight. Then what's left to live for?

Brothers at the Wadena Indoor Pool with a Diving Board
by Samuel Cole

The neighbor Heely girls were going.
Fact. We could go, too—just round up
the dough in fifteen minutes. Tick-tock.

We raced barefoot, moving a wake of
driveway dust from their door to ours.

I was tired of drawing mansions on a hill.
You were tired of playing a *yes-sire* butler.
Boyhood dryness needs summer wetness.

Male counterparts to the Heely chicks, all
of us hiding in our eyes the welts on our skin.

Their father smacked them even harder.
Their mother disappeared for weeks.
Their flower bed bred thistles & beer cans.

But they had the admission fee. We didn't.
They had an Uncle Les to drive. We didn't.

They had polka-dot beach towels. We didn't.
Hurry it up, pussies. We ain't waiting all day.
We foraged the house for a dollar-fifty fee.

I stole ninety-five cents from Mom's coat pocket.
You unearthed a quarter from beneath a rug.

I discovered a dime behind the toilet. You lifted
a dime from the bottom of the trashcan. Not enough.
Then. Ah. We dove for the nickel propping

up the kitchen table. It wobbled and tipped.
We laughed so hard. We almost missed the ride.

I wish we had. Life might be different. Somehow.

I confiscated two pennies from father's loafers.
You extracted three pennies from a sock drawer.

How little we wanted back then. Not even
two dollars. Evenness, we'd learn as men,
was not our strength, betraying us even at birth.

Our weekly allowance was the space between
parental fighting—a small gap between a large

chasm of hate that always ended in *it.*
That's it. I've had it. Shut it. Forget it. Fuck it.
We knew who we were—the byproducts of it.

The Heely hags sang and drummed the
dashboard. Uncle Les told a joke about a fag,

a priest, a bar, & a one-legged whore named
Israel Vatican. It was funny. I think. We laughed.
I think. I was distraught. I think. Were you?

It's three dollars now. You don't have enough.
Don't look at us. We barely got it ourselves.

We sat on the sidewalk, beggars without
a cup, a sign, a clue. 2 hours felt like 4½.

You guys look homeless. Let's go, doofuses.

The Heely girls squeezed chlorine
from their bangs & bragged about
backstrokes & summersaults & air

guitar & lifeguard cuties & chocolate
pudding & cheesy bacon nacho fries.

Uncle Les parked in the back of XXX.
Life's an unfair cluster-fuck boys.
Best you learn that now.

i reef
by Thomas Fucaloro

the outskirts of the summer sun
the cruelties in my mind and sensed being
has a place, hear, but after the hum
there's sobriety and all the pitfalls
that come with it. there's nothing funny
about drug abuse then why am i laughing
all the way to the blood bank. they take a pint.
i drink a pint. whatever ales ya
makes you weaker because trying to live
up to the truth staring you in the face
never made for my greatest poems.

my knees tend to buckle during these moments of honesty.

it engulfs crust thick rationalizations
that rely on the muse of the narcotic
and the ability to nonsense
and the ability to show you
i don't know what i'm doing.

Monopoly, My Brother and Money
by Martha Rand

During the summer my brother and I would sit on the porch. We read joke books and told each other jokes during the afternoons, when it was too hot to move. Sitting in butterfly chairs our dad hung from the ceiling, occasionally a slight breeze would give us a gentle spin.

My brother was a funny kid, but he was too little to really tell a good joke or riddle. It didn't matter because his enthusiasm for the telling carried his presentation.

He'd start the telling of one of his favorites, "Wanna hear a dirty joke?"

I was the big sister so I had to say, "Sure."

He'd start to giggle. He couldn't keep a straight face, and he'd told the joke so many times before that I already knew the punch line.

"A man fell into a mud puddle!" He cracked himself up. Watching him cracked me up, too. He'd roll off the chair clutching his tummy. He was so funny to watch. I had to laugh, no matter how many times he told that joke.

In the evening, we'd play marathon Monopoly games. The board would stay up for days in the stillness of summer. After dinner it was cooler. We'd re-start the game. He always won. Gleefully, he'd pretend to count his fistfuls of colored paper money.

My brother kept a piggy bank that had an alarm. Saturday mornings, he'd get up early and find the change that had fallen out of our father's pockets when Dad had taken his Friday evening nap. Sometimes he found change on the sidewalk. And, no matter what chore he was asked to do, he'd set a price.

"Go pick up your toys in the basement," my mom would direct.

"I'll do it for a dime," he'd bargain.

She'd give in.

Sometimes, my mom and I would have to "borrow" money from my brother's bank. We'd wait until my brother was outside and wouldn't be able to hear the alarm. He'd be riding his bike around the cul de sac where our house stood, or my mom would have walked him down the block to play with his friend Glenn.

I would hear the Good Humor ice cream truck pull up. Mom and I would have to break into my brother's bank for change. I'd run up the hill to get treats. We'd put his treat in the freezer until after dinner.

My brother was so little he couldn't count. If he missed some change, we could talk him out of his suspicion, because he could never actually tell us how much money he had before we'd stolen the ice cream money.

Summer after summer, he won the Monopoly games. Summer after summer, we'd laugh at his silly jokes. Until he learned to count, we'd get ice cream with the found change we stole from his piggy bank. After dinner we'd watch my little brother enjoy his treat before it was time for him to go to bed.

Summer
by Paul Beckman

The day after she turned eighteen, Autumn had her name legally changed to Summer.

Autumn was her grandmother—her mother's mother but Summer never liked her because she was too critical of her. "Any girl named after me would not be doing the things you do."

Summer's mother asked Summer not to tell her grandmother. "Autumn would have granted that request," she texted, "but Summer likes to tell things as they are."

Home from her freshman year, Summer stopped to visit her grandmother. "I don't understand how a girl with your breeding and my name could possibly wear ripped jeans, no bra and who knows what else," her grandmother said.

"A tattoo," Summer said. She turned her back and lifted her shirt to show a large Chinese letter in the small of her back.

"Just what is that all about?"

"It's the Chinese symbol for Summer, my favorite season and my new name."

"You've taken to calling yourself Summer, Autumn?"

"Better, Grandma, I've changed my name legally from Autumn to Summer. Now you won't have to complain that your namesake is trashing your good name."

"Autumn, that is the cruelest thing you could have done."

"Well, Grandma, have you ever had a visit with me when you haven't put me down or criticized me? Have you ever told me you love me or are proud of me? Have you ever introduced me to your friends at the club without making a face? The answer is no to all of these things and as I see it you don't deserve to have me share your name."

Summer received calls, emails and texts from family members berating her for changing her name. When her mother visited on parents' weekend, she told Summer that because of her actions her grandmother was cutting every family member out of her will and wouldn't change it back until she changed her name back.

"Mom, I can get along fine without Grandma's money," Summer said.

"Everyone in the family, including me, is counting on it, so you're screwing your own parents out of their inheritance. Your spite is hurting a lot of people."

"I'm not going to change my mind," Summer said, "but I am changing all of my contact information, from email to phone so I'm not bombarded by family over this anymore."

One winter day Summer answered the door and her grandmother was standing shivering in the cold, her limo running on the street. Summer invited her in, took her coat and moved a chair in front of the fireplace to warm her. "I'll make tea," she said and left the room. When she returned her grandmother was standing in her bra and panties. "What's going on, Grandma?"

"There are two Summers in our family now," her grandmother said, and turned around showing the identical tattoo. "You're the only one not after my money, and this is my way of saying I'm sorry for being so rough on you."

His Final Words
by Tom Fegan

"All killing is wrong," whimpered death row inmate Lucas James pitifully. The day had come for his fatal injection at Huntsville, Texas prison.

Texas Ranger Lewis Grinnell closed his eyes and his head dropped. Dismal ruminations returned about his investigation of the multijurisdictional slaughter of four innocent people. The murders had riveted the South Texas hamlets bordering the Gulf of Mexico and ended in Corpus Christi eight summers past. Grinnell joined the four victims' family members in the antechamber to observe Lucas's end.

Melissa Bryant, aged 20 and out of college until fall met friends for partying. She departed a small bar with a sandy-haired young man after a night of dancing to live music with the stranger. Her friends surveyed her exit with him; they winked and giggled. Her bound, multiply-stabbed and lacerated corpse was found dumped in a culvert the next morning. A prostitute and a cocktail hostess followed.

State police sent Texas Ranger Lewis Grinnell to keep local law enforcement at bay over the issue of jurisdiction. He surmised the victims were killed elsewhere and transplanted, no blood discovered surrounding the bodies; the wounds dry and sex-related. "They died begging for their lives," he grimaced. The descriptions and suspect sketches loomed in local businesses and beachfronts. One witness described Bryant and the stranger departing in a black Volkswagen, but overlooked the license plate number.

Ray Richey, an advertising executive for a local television station was the final victim. His butchered body, gagged and tied to his bed, was discovered by his housekeeper. Richey exited a Corpus Christi bar where he was a regular patron with a blonde seen chatting with him. The bartender noted James scoping them from a neighboring table. As James followed the couple out of the bar, the bartender rushed to a window and recorded the Volkswagen's plate number.

The plates lead Grinnell to James' frame home. Grinnell interrupted the suspect changing a flat tire on his black Volkswagen in his driveway, "Lucas James?" James bolted towards the lawman with a raised tire iron. The ranger snapped his revolver from his holster, "Boy, do I have to kill you?" James surrendered peacefully. His wife Lily had baited Richey in an effort to sidetrack the authorities' profile. The other murders were committed in their home. Lily claimed she fearfully aided him in the killings. The woman surrendered prior to his arrest and cut a deal-probation. "He dumped the bodies," she whimpered.

Grinnell's eyes opened. Lucas James was pronounced dead. Grinnell focused grimly on the departing families, but kept back. The State of Texas grants condemned prisoners a final statement but not a last meal of their choice. His victims never received such amenities. The final words haunted him. Killing was wrong; but so is torture. Unpardonable he reasoned; justice was served.

Like Broken Shells
by Katie Rendon Kahn

Papi took dozens of pictures
   of us that day on the beach
      when you couldn't wait
         to get back to your friends.
           I just wanted one image
      where we looked intact,
   just one frame
of unexposed negatives.
   I later held each photo
      like a broken shell,
         tried to piece the tide-turned
      edges together
   until I recognized you.
I collected the corners
   of your mouth,
      long fingers, and wisps
         of wild hair.
           I tried to fix
         your distant stare, forget
      your sharp words,
   and that you didn't
want to be there.

I sometimes walk the shore
    alone, graze over shards
        of sand dollars and conch
    shells with my toes
just like we did when you
still reached for my hand.
    You always saved the broken
        pieces we found washed up,
           you'd carry them home
    in your pockets.
    You didn't care how big
the ocean was, you said
    there was always a chance
        that you'd find the rest
         of the pieces
next time.

In the still of the deep south night
by Bruce Colbert

At rest in this warm darkness nature's vast orchestra begins
tuning for its nightly concert, first

Bayou crickets chirp in unison on the murky Bay as this
invisible maestro slowly steals from its depths, his grey
baton dripping with seaweed

retched from the eager mouths of sea snakes or eels, and

with washing waves on the tan sand, he points into the

obsidian Alabama night, and a single bull frog readies a
baritone song with

amphibian voice a magnificent

French horn perhaps passed down through the ages from the

pen of Voltaire, who believed in such things.

And so this nocturnal aria begins, sotto voce, and in the trees
insects are silenced;

A mighty croak shakes grey-green Spanish moss in Live Oaks watching, which with gnarled fingers that reach into the heavens like Welsh witches are resplendent in the clear white summer moonlight;

And as this otherworldly conductor readies his waiting orchestra, gesturing feverishly right and then left with ghostly but precise manner, this

swampy amphitheater comes alive with a hundred, or

maybe even a thousand voices: soprano, alto, baritone, and bass, all with perfect pitch, and the animal symphonic melody

weaves its way into my tired heart and the

years begin to inexorably melt away and sleep comes at last.

Rot
by Michael Koenig

In an empty bed
Tomatoes reach
Homeward, pushing out
Tiny golden globes

Plump fruit, dusty
Plunging from
A furry vine
Falls and rots
Like lemonade

The smell
Is sweet like
Plastic and
Every one
Of them is
Spoilt.

Avocado Sandwiches on a July Afternoon

by Joanne Jagoda

We had been nervously waiting at home expecting a long drawn-out labor as our daughter had to be induced, so we were stunned and overjoyed when she called us herself to say that she was holding the baby in her arms. The little guy had made an impressively quick, uneventful entrance. We rushed to the hospital to greet our fifth grandchild, hug our heroic daughter and proud son-in-law. It is an awesome thrill to hold a newborn and we were smitten by the tiny blond bundle. After spending several hours with the new little family, we left them to get a sandwich at the Whole Foods down the street from the hospital.

We felt blessed that everything had gone well and the baby was healthy but our joy was tempered by the fact I had been diagnosed with breast cancer a few days before. My diagnosis was shocking because I did not have a family history and had always been very healthy until my routine mammogram showed something which needed to be looked at a second time. The radiologist was not particularly alarmed and said I could wait a few months. A new doctor I saw felt a lump in my breast and recommended I go for the second mammogram sooner. This time, based on the body language and grunts of the radiologist, I knew I was in trouble. A few days later, a surgical biopsy confirmed what I suspected and from that moment I was thrust into frightening uncharted territory. I immediately needed to find a surgeon, and despite initial insurance hassles, fortunately was able to get an appointment with a surgeon at one of the finest medical institutions in the country, UCSF, where I stayed for all my treatment. On that joyous day in July celebrating my grandson's birth, I had no idea what lay ahead for me. Besides the lumpectomy I would have in August, I would face nine months of grueling chemotherapy and radiation.

We shared our tuna sandwich on a French roll sitting outside in the warm July afternoon sun on wooden tables, but I could barely eat. A few tables away, I noticed an older gentleman, in his late seventies, dressed neatly in khakis, a polo shirt and wearing a Giants cap. He had a stack of bread slices in front of him, 6 or 8, a knife and several avocados. I watched as he meticulously carved pieces of a lush avocado, then placed them like a mosaic on half a piece of the bread. He folded over the other half and voraciously ate his avocado sandwiches one after another working through the whole stack.

I was fascinated and mesmerized. I was envious. I imagined in my mind he was able to lose himself in the ritual dance of making his sandwiches. I wanted to forget my cancer diagnosis. I wanted my old life back. *Mr. Avocado man… can you show me how you make your sandwiches?*

Scrape
by Jon Dietrick

Most people scrape. You hear it, in the morning after a big snow: first the dead quiet, then the "beep beep" of a plow backing up. Then shovels cutting ice and snow. Then all this scraping. The car's running and they're scraping the shit out of their windshields with these jagged, hard, plastic things. You pay $20,000 for your Honda Fit or whatever and then you scrape the fucking window like it's a Dodge fucking Dart.

Me, here's what I do: I get up. I start the car. I go back inside. I have a cup of coffee and a cigarette. I let the car do the work.

They're called defrosters. They do the work for you: that is, they defrost your fucking windshield. They melt the ice, the snow, all that shit. Ten, fifteen minutes later, you go out there: done. Maybe you want to hit the windshield washer button, run the wipers a little. Maybe, OK, brush the half-melted snow off your windshield (gently), if you really need to do something with your arms. Whatever. The point is: your windshield is clean, you can see out the fucking thing, and you didn't scratch the shit out of it with a piece of hard plastic from fucking CVS. Come summer, you aren't going to notice all these tiny annoying fucking scratches all over your glass.

And: your car's warm. Your fucking car is warm. Your hands aren't all frostbitten, your skin isn't all red and shit. Cause I got the eczema. Everyone in my family has it. I go out there and scrape in the fucking ice and cold, even if I wanted to, if I didn't care about scratching my windshield, I lost my fucking marbles, whatever – my hands are like raw meat. From the eczema. But I don't scrape. I start the car, I go back inside. Have an orange juice. Take a shit. Whatever. Whole time, my car does the work.

I tell people. But you know what? It doesn't matter. Cause they're gonna scrape that shit anyway. You know why? Because they have issues that they're repressing. They're working out their anger. On their fucking $40000 Lexus. Scraping and cursing and thinking about, I don't know, their kid isn't talking to them, they don't love their wife, they want to take it up the ass. They have cancer. Their kid has cancer. Whatever. Life took a shit on them. Then on top of that life dumps a bunch of snow and fucking ice on their car. And they have to get up, in the dark, and scrape. But the truth is they're happy to have to scrape. Cause if they didn't do that – what? They'd lie there and think about their lives. The scraping, it's something to do.

But not me. I let the car do the work. They're called fucking defrosters. Use them.

Approaching 40
by Chris Gillies

Here I stand, facing a fierce blue sky. It's summer. I'm melting. Eyes cast to the distant hue of trees and rolling hills, while in front of me stand three Black Angus heifers too hot to move, apart from the swish of a tail to detach a stubborn fly. I stare at them, they stare at me and chew some grassy remnant.

My ears are used to the city sounds of sirens, cars, people, and the hectic pace, and can't quite adjust to the silence here. My ears strain against the nothing. It's unsettling for a moment. Calming the next.

Looking down, the result of driving for hours in the heat was obvious as my right arm sunburnt red, while my left office pale. An ex, a smile, a touch and a rush all led me to where I am now, and I'm thankful. Oh what a smile.

Once again, I'm living in my thoughts and staring into the abyss. I need to come back to reality.

I step into the kitchen, looking at the thermometer by the old wooden door – it's approaching 40 and it's not yet 8am.

This is not my house. It's Ben's, a friend, who lives alone; I've come for the weekend. The house is old, its textured timbers recall a time when families once lived under its eaves and worked the land that surrounds.

My silence is broken, as Ben steps on the kitchen's faded green lino.

"I always feel uneasy on days like this," he says, a worried expression on his usual cheery face. "There will be someone somewhere, who should know better, who will fuck up and set fire to something."

I nod my concern, and look over the dry grass paddock. My mind paints a picture of a rampaging fire engulfing the old cottage in which we stand.

In my imagination, Ben and I are sitting in an old enamel bath with the Angus heifers, filled with water and navigating our way through the blazing inferno.

Rub-a-Dub-Dub two men, three heifers, no bull, in a tub.

Coves
by Piet Nieuwland

The mermaids at Langs Beach
Slip and dive into the high tide
Speaking Swedish in pink, multicultural Maori
Singing black Californian, polka dot Dutch
Laughing French coffee accents and hints of Chinese spice
Scarlet English blondes and Indian ebony golds
In a breeze as warm as Bream Bay waves
Through tangled pohutukawa shade
The summer altar of beach ritual and display
Inclines in, to shelly sand recline
Scent of salt, soft sweet spot of sun on the back
Sunglass peering, sunscreen spreading all over
The islands just over the horizon
Curves curve away just enough to
Sea foam hiss and turquazure blues

I'm pretty hot
by Erica Gerald Mason

so when we moved to Georgia
it was late June
almost July
but when we first visited
to go house hunting
it was February
and the temperature was 60 degrees
and it felt like heaven compared to
the 30-degree temperature in Indiana
and everyone in both Georgia and Indiana told us
how hot Georgia would be in the summertime
and maybe we should try to move earlier
so we could acclimate our bodies to the temperature change
but we laughed and rolled our eyes and thought they were
making things
too complicated

so we moved in the first week of summer

and when we stepped out of the moving van

I felt as if the entire state of Georgia had slapped me across

the face

it was unbearable

I turned to my husband

and saw that his entire face was a shower curtain of sweat

that first summer I became the patron saint of hotness

I said oh my God it's so hot

more than I said my own name

and when people asked me how I was doing

I always said

I'm pretty hot.

Nines and Nineties
by Glenn A. Bruce

We were nine. The creek called.
Salamanders—watch the red ones! They're poisonous!
They weren't.
They can kill you if you touch them!
They couldn't.
We picked them up, eventually
                                    and lived.
Boy, did we live!
The creek was alive in summer.
The water was cool, but not cold;
clear, and revealing:
crawdaddies like tiny, feisty lobsters,
their short but sharp pincers snapping;
brown salamanders, black salamanders,
tiny trout and water spiders, both darting,
frightened of our huge, looming presence.
Harmless! We were harmless.
We didn't kill; we cherished.
We took no life—only stones. Gems!
Quartz awaited every visit,
Milky, smoky, glassy—but pristine,
millions of years old,
ready for the taking
                        and we took them.

Now, it's all lost.
Even in the headwaters,
just feet below the source spring,
any salamander is rare.
The reds have been gone for decades,
taking the crawdaddies with them
                              forever.
We stole all the good quartz,
left them in a drawer somewhere
for our mothers to throw away
when we moved out, or went to college,
or got married, or moved away, or
                        just gave up.
To end up in some landfill,
back to the earth, but not really.
Now, we're all ninety. The creek calls.
But we can't find our way back.
They've all dried up and vanished,
But we have remained, somehow,
                        and lived.

Jack Daniels
by Sara Petersen

Iowa. Summertime. The heady scent of whiskey and cologne permeate Grandpa's welcome hug. Tom Jones croons to us ("Pussycat, pussycat I love you, yes I dooooo") from the Buick's speakers. Shiny maroon leather seats, packs of peppermint gum tucked in the center console. We cruise the flat streets of Schleswig's mile-large downtown and swap stories with Grandpa's cronies at the bank and the post office. Jolly laughter and big full voices. The men are tanned and healthy, wearing worn jeans and chambray shirts. The shops and businesses are chateau style, straight out of Switzerland or Tudor England – like they're made of gingerbread.

We kids hike downtown to Grandpa's Pump 'N Shop and drink pop from glass bottles, proudly telling the clerk to "charge it on Bill." Our Grandpa is a big man in town. He has a bar in the basement where there's a plastic jackpot toy, with a little man's head that pops up like a jack-in-the-box and spits water at you when you pull the lever down to see if you can get three of a kind. There's a murky green shag carpet and a fuzzy velour recliner. The wall is papered with a panoramic view of New England foliage.

My dad and Uncle Joel drink with their high school buddies. Grandpa loves every second of telling them they're full of shit. The boisterous bond of liquor and beer wraps us in a warm embrace of laughter and bonhomie. My grandmother smiles tolerantly at her big, handsome sons and her larger-than-life husband as the ice clinks in her

Manhattan. Blondness everywhere.

We sit on the porch at night, stroking our bare feet lazily along the fake, green turf floor. We watch the fireflies and stars blend into one swathe of sparkle over the cornfields. The adults rock gently on old, iron porch furniture, sipping drinks and chatting. Their conversation lulls us as we eat our vanilla ice cream with raspberries from Grandma's garden in the cozy fog of cigar smoke.

Christmas time. My sister and I gallop down the stairs to the basement. We're drinkers now ourselves, and 5 o'clock cocktail hour is *so* much more fun. We slice our lemons and limes, squeeze them into the ice filled glasses. We pour Petersen sized shots of vodka (never measured) and top them off with splashes of tonic. After the tumor is detected, Grandpa is cut off from whiskey and confined to red wine. Grandma hides the hard stuff in the sewing room closet, so Megan and I mix our cocktails amongst spindles and needles and velcro.

New Hampshire. Summertime. Grandma and Grandpa are visiting. As I dash into the kitchen for a glass of water, I bump into Grandpa gulping whiskey from the bottle. His bumbling shame makes me ache. I feign ignorance and hurry from the room.

Alcohol is poison, but our booze is golden and family and laughter and Jack Daniels is Grandpa.

Indian Summer
by Martin Christmas

Toddler,
sand running,
pulled back by her
young laughing father.

Dolphin,
ragged finned,
lazily circling its mate
in a passionate adagio.

Three golden rays,
linger across
the luminous horizon,
signalling day's end.

Ubiquitous seagulls,
parallel to the beach,
winging silently seaward
to invisible roosts.

Surf crashing,
an endless barreling
along the flat sand,
like expressive steam trains.

Silhouette shapes,
walking, running
talking, looking, pausing
in soft communion with the light.

A moving panorama,
surreal dinner setting
ruptured but intact.
Last notes of Summer's song.

Summerfall
by Tim Philippart

Living on the edge summer,
with leaves creeping toward fullness,
and shadows near their deepest,
the anticipation on this cusp, is not,

Like that in Winter,
when it's too long and cold,
to anticipate anything more,
than snowflakes and frostbite.

Even, early spring's cautious buds,
and crocus scouts,
live in fear,
of winter's frozen grip.

Then, on the thin line
at the border of spring and summer,
anticipation blinks,
into June.

Leaves unfurl,
grass reminds the mower,
dandelions puff seeds,
and for a moment, it's summer.

Right then, at that instant,
Summer ends.
Long-term dread,
replaces all anticipation.

I don't believe in summer,
until I step in it.
Then, I fear my next footfall,
slips in the snow.

In the Beginning, Good Always Overpowered Taxidermied Chipmunks and Free Frosting Wednesdays at Applebee's
by David S. Atkinson

Summer? I remember Summer. She was that hot chic in my zero gravity creative writing class in high school. Not sure why they did that, since it didn't improve the writing at all, but it sure made it difficult to get lines down on paper. All the coffee and goatees kept floating away. Mostly, I spent the class periods ogling Summer… who didn't have a goatee anyway. I think she had coffee, but that might have been a mixture of Crystal Clear Pepsi and old pencil shavings instead.

It was kind of hard to tell from where I was bolted in.

I remember running into her at a National Pickle Week drinking party that some amateur bowling alley mechanic enthusiasts on the school bus invited me to. They were only trying to get me to vote for the Mann Act, but it was nice to be invited for once… even if the cessation of death three months prior had caused fermentation to stop and thus no one could drink because there wasn't any liquor to be had.

We still had fun watching that Robin Hood animal cartoon and wrecking whoever's house they had borrowed for the party, though that did lead to Hulk Hogan biting Summer's ass.

I mean, even if she did bend over in those Dukes of Hazzard commemorative denim shorts and put it right in his face, that was still no excuse. He wasn't supposed to be playing a heel, and should have asked permission first regardless.

No, wait... that was Mimi's ass that Hogan bit, not Summer's. Don't know why I'm talking about that if it didn't have anything to do with Summer. Mimi was a knockout too, but she certainly wasn't Summer... as all girls who weren't Summer weren't.

Everybody knows Summer.

Though I don't mean biblically, since she wasn't comfortable with that outside of Tennessee. Sure, there was that time the police found her with Abraham and his child on the hill by that altar, claiming God said to kill the kid, but you can't call the situation biblical simply due to a few similarities. There's lots of things in the Bible and we'll never get anywhere if we start labeling everything as biblical that bears any faint resemblance at all.

It just isn't the same.

But Summer though, Summer was a cool chic. If it hadn't been for that year after high school when she took the interim president emeritus of ConAgra hostage in the Leavenworth Street 7-11 to protest pudding prices, I'd wonder what she was up to these days. I may not be the smartest man, but I know when the NSA makes it safer not to ask.

Even for Summer.

Riding the Earth's Rotation
by Janet Malotky

Lie awake on your back in the grass
in the grass with dandelions asleep
with the smell of freshly cut and
barely damp on the nape,
shins and shoulders draped in the shawl of night
eyes afloat in half-closed pools
of touch me

It must be night
black as a black water lake and
astounding with stars,
stars reaching down with
their threads of distilled dream
like tiny lightning
and raising from the skin
filaments of desire

There will be fireflies
measuring out the dimensional night
with their unpredictable patterns of flight,
that rivet in their dark interludes,
their code calling down the stars

There must be the touch of
fingertips on the breast bone
trailing with the bare pressure
of an urge and a need condensed
and held in a bubble of heat
in the throat of a loon
and ready

This touch must move,
trailing up between star and firefly
across the skin of the night
drawing them down
to a focused burn of light
a black hole
with the rings of Saturn expanding

And there must not be words
though the world is a round word at such times
round as a vowel and plump,
a plum word exhaled by dandelions
closed and sleeping
a mouth shape made by stars and fireflies
through the summer night.

Red-Eye Flight
by Lana Bella

your red-eye flight dipped into
the wide stretched asphalt
of Fairbanks,
negotiated a crooked return
over the drenched runway—
the sky rust veined
with split red of second warmth,
pressing with its ill carny lights—
you felt the rise and fall
of your chest as it sped up
before it slowed,
whose wings parted the sky
searching for pockets of moonlight
where your heart still beat
maelstrom into the topography
of this long lost summer,
yet this delusion will recede,
because soon, you will remember
you can't wither anywhere else but here—

Highway Sketch
by Susan Tally

If summer ends in classical coda,
Let July and August be a country ballad—
Radio playing in a vehicle for two,
The only couple for miles around—
Friends forever with the windows rolled down.
July is wrapped in the American flag,
Then violin and woodwind greens
Billow in August's plaid sleeves.

Lying on the Deck
by A.J. Huffman

of the sailboat, feeling the rise and fall
of the current beneath me, I close my eyes,
imagine I am flying. Wind surrounds me,
I am feather. I am wing. Two strokes then holding
pattern, I let momentum carry me higher, higher
until I lose all definition, become one with the warming
eye of the sun.

Summer morning, Sandy Bay
by Mercedes Webb-Pullman

Pre-dawn peak hour.
Little blue penguins stream
from under the bach like
suit-wearing shift workers
power-walking
to the office.

Over the shingle road they hurry,
down through sand dunes,
speed increasing
nearer the sea.

Teeter-tottering
wings outstretched
they rush
to hurl themselves
into their work.

Summer Highland Falls
by Michael Webb

It is early May, but it already feels like mid-summer, a hot dry wind turning my throat arid as I breathe. The game started at 4:00, but even this late day sun feels strong. I'm watching the pitcher for Highland High School, a kid named Ferguson, make short work of us, allowing only two hits and striking out 10 so far. I watch him, shaggy hair sticking out under his dusty white cap, his face blank and smooth, his high cheekbones covered with black paint, a shadow of stubble on his chin, looking in for the sign. His uniform, green and white, looks like it was tailored, smooth and taut across the length of him. I can picture him wearing a tuxedo, or a t-shirt, clothes draping over the ridges of muscle he carries. He wears very high socks, his calves an expanse of color on his long legs. He glides more than he moves, straightening up to his full height, and then twisting and turning and exploding at the batter, his arm blurring as it moves.

I take my place at the plate. I focus my attention on him, standing in the sun, his body turning, beginning his windup. I focus at where I expect the ball to be. I start swinging, years of muscle memory turning into my own load, coil, and release, my black bat flashing through, my hips rotating smoothly, the delicate ping of the ball hitting square. I knew I had hit it on the screws, as the saying goes, and I was starting to run to first, when I heard a second sound, a soft smack like dropping an orange onto a sidewalk, followed by a third, a sudden intake of breath. I was still running, but I

112

slowed and stopped when I saw their first baseman's face. A tall, thick-waisted Hispanic kid, he looked like he was about to vomit.

I looked, and Ferguson was down, stretched out flat on the grass, his feet still on the dirt of the mound behind him. He looked dead. I wanted to scream or shake, but I stood in the baseline, watching first one teammate, then another, take an uncertain step, and then another, and then the team and their fat bearded coach were there, surrounding him, a red first aid kit on the green grass. The game and the score were forgotten, the ball discarded and alone, and when they turned Ferguson over, I could see blood smearing his hard face, his jaw and cheek already swelling, his eyes closed with the pain. I stared, helpless, as they led him off the field, a warrior felled, and I wanted to cry as if the ball had hit my own face.

One Season Down Under
by Alex Robertson

No respite for Australia
Amidst December and beyond
Unrepentant warmer climes
In both tropics and the temperate zones
Seasonal differences apparent
Summer:
    a warm heat in Europe
Nothing like the island continent
Shades of Dante's Inferno
And the various circles of hell
In the days past the solstice

Owner occupiers chill their homes
These inside quarters are altered states
With box conditioners or split systems
Plugging away against the radiation
    with cellular or open plan structures
Cooled to half the heat outside
As if unnecessary ice blocks are formed
For this maximum comfort gone overboard

A loved sunburnt country
Ochres adorning the hummocks
And rust covered landscapes
Desert baked in midday sun
Pilfered for ore by miners
Carted seaward to be purified
Now fired in the forge
To different temperatures altogether
In Whyalla, an oxidized red dust town

Much of South Australia swelters
Buckled rail tracks and liquid tar roads
Thermometers near bursting point
Well over 100 in the old scale
Above body heat
Looking for a breather

The seashore becomes a temporary relief
As in the West
   just what the 'Doctor ordered
Salt water dips worth the wait
Towels spread under the jetty on tepid sand
Sunlight protected in the shadows
And when the beach cools in the evening
Almost balmy nights prevail
Amid sweat and mosquito coils
Retiring to ceiling fans and cotton sheets
For the renter's choice of relief
In a mid-summer's delight

Morose Code
by Devin Taylor

In such suchness we are scripted
such: Dots and dashes;

dashed-dots/dotted-dashes—
nothing less, nothing more...

equivocated in scripts
which run their course

like stocking seams.
Us, basking in yesterdays'

dashes of summer sun,
conjuring comforting

algorithmic luminescence
eloquated in codes,

programmed loops. for(;;)
Obsolescence dusts

our machine parts;
The Motherboard

{(through its own)}
births our demise.

Mr. Lonely Hearts
by Gay Degani

His writing traded in gooey gold sunsets, magic mailboxes on lakes, covered bridges fronting burnished Vermont. He sold millions of copies to sad-eyed secretaries whose flings with bosses ended in wine-by-the-box tears in front of *Wheel of Fortune,* thirty-somethings who blew their opportunities for that very special first time with Mr. Wonderful down on the beach in summer with dudes named Ronnie Doan, Tommy T, and algebra teachers like Mr. Fletcher. Middle-aged marrieds, great aunts, grandmas, third cousins, men with soft hearts, these sad souls made up his clan and he was grateful.

Grateful for his upscale beachside condo on an exclusive Florida key, his Wally powerboat, the Maserati that looked like a Toyota Corolla, but cost a hundred thousand dollars more, and *yet* he was not happy, not happy at all. He would roll around in bed until noon, then get up in the worst heat of the day, sit on the beach in a white plastic chair, notepad in hand, his skin becoming dark as coffee, wrinkled as his morning bowl of prunes. He'd bake there, his mind castigating him for his stupidity, his lack of talent, his shallowness. He did this for months until hurricane season drove him inside and he booted his Mac.

He knew this could be a new beginning if he chose it to be. He'd promised himself that he could write something true and sincere if he gave himself time. Why not? Others had before him. He didn't have to be a Faulkner or a Joyce.

He could settle for Updike. Franzen. Even Dennis Lehane.

He pounded, caressed, battered his keyboard until winds reached 80 miles an hour. The windows rattled. Palm trees groaned. He reread his last tortured paragraph. Groaned. Maybe if he added a covered bridge, a time-traveling attic. He shrugged, shook his head, and thought: *Better launch my boat toward the mainland, check in at the Four Seasons Palm Beach, open a catalogue of Thomas Kincaid paintings, and begin my next best-selling tome.*

The Point
by Cynthia Leslie-Bole

My legs, furred with blonde hair, pump as I run. Twigs criss-cross my tanned skin with scrapes as I sprint past. I feel honest soil crusted between my toes and smell the must of my unwashed hair baking in the summer sun.

I zigzag through grass tall enough to graze my armpits, dart by my grandparents' house under camouflage of shrubbery, clamber over hummocks of moss, then scramble along a knife-edge path that demarcates a ravine on one side and a rocky cliff that plunges into Lake Erie on the other. I come finally to The Point, a jutting overhang of dirt clutched tightly by the roots of a towering maple and carpeted with grass. I flop down, lean back against the maple's rough trunk, and drink in my destination.

This place is accessible only to the young, the agile, the heedless; it is a point of solitude levitating above a sparkling, heaving Great Lake. The honor of admittance to The Point can be won only by trekking and risking and knowing the secret way. It is a point of view open to select child initiates, and once there, a vast new vista opens inside and out.

Knowing the tree could release its grip, topple, and crash down the pebbled cliff makes my senses alert, my mind sharp to danger, and my body aware of its throb of life. Knowing that no one has any idea where I am, that grownups couldn't make it to The Point even if they wanted to, contributes an existential excitement to the hum of the place. Knowing that my tiny spark of consciousness perceives the vastness unobserved, that the watcher isn't being watched, opens me up. Knowing that for this moment I am who I am, with no requirements, no judgments, no promises, sends me sailing into the expanse of lake and sky, only to be called back by the caw of a gull. I surge out again into a morphing cumulus cloud, then crash back in with a roiling breaker. The freedom of dissolved boundaries carries me inward and outward in waves that mirror the fresh water below. Time expands into irrelevance, and I sit forever, watching, feeling, and just being.

Eventually, though, forever must collapse back into a specific moment, and my stomach rumbles, my arms prickle with goosebumps as clouds erase the sun, and the iron in my blood responds to the pull of home. Questions inevitably begin plucking the feathers from my flight. "Does anyone notice I'm gone? Do they care where I am? How long would it take them to notice if I never came home? What if I fell down the cliff and died and nobody ever knew?"

I try to answer "I don't care" with a mental shrug and believe it. But already I'm standing up, dusting off my frayed denim shorts, and turning to lope down the trail, anxious again to trade the now too-big, secret viewpoint for my small, shared world.

Finally Understanding
Entropy in Summer
by Ben Pitts

When the wind is free,
grill heat bends things
into waves.

Slight light in the trees
shadow the row of dandelions:
snap them in the middle
feel the break,
blow.
The white puffs float—
a reminder of snow
white sheets,
months ago ya' know,
covered all of this.

My pores open
to the slow stun
of sun off water,
but I can't remember
when the world
was junglejimmed
with painted iron.

See the children flop
around in clear lakes?
Can't think of anytime
when anything
made me happy
like that.

Summer Karma
(a found poem)
by Mark Hudson

Yesterday I went into a copy center, and a
senior citizen wanted to make a copy of a
manuscript, a novel she wrote.

As she pulled it out of her bag, she
became aware that her dog had crapped all over it.

They still tried to make a copy of it anyhow,
but secretly, I found this amusing.

Then, at the local art store, it was the first day
of a back to school sale, and I went to check it out.
A man in a black kilt or dress, eager to take advantage
of the sale, clutched tons of art supplies in his hands,
and knocked over an art display that scattered into pieces.

Once again, I was secretly amused. But today,
it was my turn. I was at school, about to add
color to a drawing, and I pulled my colored
pencils out of my portfolio case, and they
went flying all over the dusty floor.

The lady who was the studio monitor said
"Is the music too loud? Should I put something on that is
       mellow?" And I said, "No, I made a mistake, it's
nobody's fault."
       But when I made a mistake, nobody laughed.
       All three occurrences could happen to anybody.
       But it's more likely to happen in summer,
when sweat cuts off circulation to brains,
and it's the year 2013, and someone once
said thirteen is bad luck, so it must be.

The Last Day of Summer
by Kate Hall

You said you were with me when I swam, but I remember being alone that afternoon. I had stripped off to my underwear so I could play mermaid in the mermaid pool. At the last minute I remembered to remove my moonstone necklace, the little delicate silver one. I left my moonstones in a shallow depression in the rock beside the mermaid pool. You remember that crater as being much deeper.

"Like the size and shape of my two cupped hands."

Your memory is probably more reliable than mine. Maybe. Even so, that reef offered little protection for anything not fused to it by root or shell or fossilised bone. When I finished swimming that day I made my usual crossing back over the rocks, shook the sand off my dress and wandered home. And when the tide rose that evening, when I drove back to the beach, racing the rising sea, hoping desperately for a miracle, I knew my necklace was gone.

We went out that night after work, as we usually did. I must have been hungover in the morning but at that age it hardly registered. I remember being up at dawn and trailing behind you as you led the way across the freshly uncovered rocks to the point. You were the only moving being in my line of vision, and your long legs and dark curls and the delicate wind ripple of your dress are so tightly woven into my memory of that place that I still see you there today, phantom-flickering in and out of the frame.

I had woken to a series of irate text messages from my boyfriend, all of which I ignored. But that morning, after the miracle, high on the wonder of what seemed the clearest sign yet, I finally made my decision.

"I have to tell him it's over," I said, burying my feet in the wet sand.

You just smiled. Back then I thought that the sea and the sunrise and the beauty of the reef were agents of change, but I know now that you were the catalyst; the alchemical secret in my first real metamorphosis. I stood there, the ocean in surround sound and the waves licking my ankles, and I felt in my bones the seismic grating of something making way for something else.

So I guess I'm writing this to thank you. For driving me to the point at daybreak. For making me follow you out onto the rocks, for being there when the new sunlight caught my moonstones and I looked down and there they were, curled in the same place, cradled by the same cupped handful of rock and waiting, defying tides and currents and the greedy fingers of mermaids for me to swoop on them with an elated cry and hold them up, triumphant and awestruck, so that you would see and be the other terminal in the conduit of my delight.

Rain Shower
by Allan J. Wills

Snails must sense time differently to us, I wonder. Waking after an afternoon nap, I watch as a herd of snails, alarmed by the fierce sun returning after the summer cloudburst, retreat towards the shade. They know well enough to get the heck out of the hot sun. Just the execution of the retreat lacks haste. Wouldn't it be frustrating if snail thoughts were way ahead of snail athletics?

Why do we leave having children so late? When we look for the right partner and wait for the right circumstances it takes an eon of time. Sometimes we find our biological machinery is flawed or mismatched. Yet our thoughts are in place and our expectations high.

While we can still imagine, we are never too old to raise children. There are many stories to sustain our hope. Think of the happy old couple finding Momotaro springing from a peach floating in a river in the Japanese folk story *Peach Boy*; or the lives of the old bamboo cutter and his wife enriched by the foundling in *The Princess and the Moon*.

Between us on the bed our three-year-old son sleeps, and in her cot our baby girl sleeps too. These two are the products of our gametes, assisted reproduction technology, good fortune, and a whole lot of love. We are ancients as far as parents go: already feeling the beginnings of autumn in our bones. In real life, as in folk tales, wherever they come from, children are a miraculous gift.

A Khan is Crowned
in Atlantic City
by Embe Charpentier

Ring bell, *please bell.* Only five more minutes. Don't let her catch me. But Mrs. Heinemann moves fast in my direction. I keep my eyes turned away from Precious' desk.

Mrs. Heinemann's face is red as a stop sign as she takes my final exam. "Cheating again, Dontavious? Don't you know better? I always catch you," she whispers. Is she smiling?

Yep. One of those I-gotcha-good smiles.

I'm already failing. That's why I cheated. I don't have to see my report card to know where I'll be headed this summer. Every eight o'clock, I'll be in credit recovery with every other failure in the ninth grade. Not just Algebra I, but World History, too.

No working basketball camp. No swag, no cheddar, no meeting Isaiah Thomas.

I'll hear Mama's voice as I escape out the back door. "Cheaters never prosper, Dontavious. I *told* you that."

The air conditioning at Strawberry Mansion High never works right, but when it's ninety, you broil like ribs on a Weber grill. Nothing decorates the classroom walls. Every mumbled word echoes off the cinderblock walls. The custodians locked all the computers and printers in the media center, because in this neighborhood, you can't take chances. But all ninety-six cameras and the metal detectors work just fine, all the time.

"Genghis Khan wasn't as negative an influence as previously believed," Heinemann reminds us. "He allowed religious freedom among his people and abolished torture."

"Then how come we're being tortured now?" Jackson yells. Snickers all around. Dude has it right.

"Should've thought of that last September." Heinemann's tart reply doesn't shut us up, so she sits down at her desk. "Copy your handouts into your notebook. No talking."

As if. "Dontavious!" Genesis Clark whispers.

I keep writing, head down. But Genesis, pretty as a Cali sunset, with thick braids knotted in a head bun, throws a tiny paper ball onto my desk.

"Gimme your number," the paper says.

I scribble it down and toss the ball back. My phone chirps.

Skip day tomorrow reads the screen.

Hell, any guy with twenty-four wives like Genghis Khan took a day off now and then. Why not me?

I meet Genesis a few streets from the bus stop. She dangles car keys and points to a red-pink Corolla as old as she is.

"Get in," she says. She holds a learner's permit in her hand. I hope it's hers.

I grab the door handle, then stop. "Who else is skippin' with us?"

"Nobody. We're goin' to Atlantic City."

I hear her best Rihanna impression for half of the sixty miles we spend on the highway. The car bucks at sixty-five, but she floors it anyway. "A good first date?" she asks.

I live in my smile.

Sapphire skies blend into a sparkling ocean. I lay back on blazing sand. "Who'd win more in a casino, Sun Tzu or Confucius?" I say.

"I dare you to ask Heinemann tomorrow, D." Then she gives me an all-conquering kiss.

Heartless Summer
by Ruby Ewens

She wiped the cold gel from her stomach with a tissue. The registrar was efficient and friendly, but she smiled too much.

"Do you want to see the ultrasound?"

"No."

She had been preparing herself for this question, sucking on the chalky mints and watching the Foxtel sideshow in the waiting room. It was election time. The faces of politicians pensive as she tried to unravel her shock. A young boy next to her sat swathed in thick bandage up to his thigh.

"I think it's broken." He was optimistic.

Her breasts ached, already tight with milk. Her sweaty back stuck to the thin plastic seat, and she didn't have the heart to congratulate him.

Walking the gritty streets, she picked out the pregnant women in the crowds, their stomachs taut under sheer cotton dresses.

She anticipated the questions from her friends and family: "*Who's the father? Why were you not more careful?*"

It was a relief to shelter at home. She exhausted her Sick Leave, unable to face work, feeling strained and wilted. Summer didn't help: she lay turtled on her back, the brackish stench of sleep and tears in the sheets. Her dreams were slick, swimming through currents, caught in the filaments of time: recurring and unsatisfying, chasing a little girl through steep hills. Terrifying how much she looked like her lover, the father. They would fall together: blue eyes, her hair the colour of dry wheat.

She arrived at the Clinic early, a small brown house on the edge of the city. Men clustered at the gate, collars against a hot wind, placards featuring a foetus bobbing in a thin tomato soup. Aggressive but distracted: she slipped past unnoticed and entered a hushed reception where everyone sat in sad, docile silence.

She blew her nose. Someone thought she was crying.

"Are you okay?" they asked her.

Her words sharp. "Just a cold."

The TV soft in the corner: Trump stabbing the air, declaring punishment to women who choose abortion. A crumpled pamphlet from her doctor wet in her hands. The story of being knocked out and sucked out by a tube the size of a hens' night penis straw.

She looked at the photo snapped on her phone that morning; the width of her body caught in the bathroom mirror, the white dough of her hips preparing for carriage.

It took her a while to respond to the nurse calling her name. Surfacing from one dream or another, the fear of falling. She made eye contact with the nurse and stood up, nodding *yes, yes, yes, I'm coming* as she slowly crossed the room.

1st snapshot of the day
by Ruth Sabath Rosenthal

reproduced in sepia

mother frowning
in alzheimers' beige
beside father
in dark brown and
a bit of white off
to the side that was
my wedding gown
as i floated across
a deep brown lawn

reproduced in color

mother frowning
in pink beside father
in navy and a bit of white
off to the side that was
my wedding gown
as i floated across
a summer lawn on a day
mother's alzheimers
couldn't color blue

Summer's End
by Sally Reno

Temperatures don't change much and leaves don't do anything they don't usually do, but when the waters inside the reef fill with strings of pearly fish spawn, when the smallest bright birds leave the island ahead of the winds, when the green dog is the last star left in the sky before dawn, then summer is almost gone.

And wasn't it lovely to lie in a hammock under water that was tied to the back of a houseboat on houseboat row; then, after sunset, to roll off into a dinghy stuffed with sleeping bags and row across the bight to snuggle in the boat and watch a movie at the Island Drive-In? It was.

We didn't understand we were killing the golden goose. When the drive-in closed forever the broken-hearted old guy who owned the place left a message on his machine: "The Island Drive-In is temporarily closed while we have our equipment re-scrutinated." Feeling like assholes and just for laughs, we called the number again and again and we thought about dying and the fugitive nature of lovely things.

Authors

Alex Reece Abbott

writes across genres, forms and hemispheres. Published here and there, Alex's literary historical novel *The Helpmeet* was a 2016 Greenbean Irish Novel Fair winner. Her contemporary novel, *Last of the Lucky Country*, shortlisted for the 2015 Northern Crime Competition. A Northern Crime Competition and Arvon Prize winner, her short fiction often shortlists, including for the Sunday Business Post/Penguin Short Story Prize, and Bridport Prize. She barely blogs at www.alexreeceabbott.info.

David S. Atkinson

is the author of *Apocalypse All the Time* (forthcoming 2017), *Not Quite so Stories*, *The Garden of Good and Evil Pancakes* (2015 National Indie Excellence Awards finalist in humor), and *Bones Buried in the Dirt* (2014 Next Generation Indie Book Awards finalist, First Novel <80K). His writing appears in *Bartleby Snopes*, *Grey Sparrow Journal*, *Atticus Review*, and others. His writing website is http://davidsatkinsonwriting.com/.

Paul Beckman

was one of the winners in the *Queen's Ferry* 2016 Best of the Small Fictions. His 200+ stories are widely published in print and online in the following magazines amongst others: *Connecticut Review*, *Raleigh Review*, *Litro*, *Playboy*, *Pank*, *Blue Fifth Review*, *Flash Frontier*, *Matter Press*, *Pure Slush*,

Metazen, Boston Literary Magazine, Jellyfish Magazine, Thrice Fiction and *Literary Orphans*. His latest collection, *Peek*, weighed in at 65 stories and 120 pages. Find his website at www.paulbeckmanstories.com.

Lana Bella

is a Pushcart nominee and the author of two chapbooks, *Under My Dark* (Crisis Chronicles Press, 2016) and *Adagio* (forthcoming from Finishing Line Press). She has had her poetry and fiction featured in over 200 journals, including *California Quarterly, Chiron Review, Columbia Journal, Poetry Salzburg Review, Plainsongs, The Writing Disorder, Third Wednesday*, and many others. She resides in the US and the coastal town of Nha Trang, Vietnam, where she is a mom of two far-too-clever frolicsome imps.

R. Bremner

of Glen Ridge via Lyndhurst, NJ, USA, is a former cab driver, truck unloader, security guard, computer programmer, and vice-president at Citibank. Ron writes of dead kings and many things he can't define, incense, peppermints, and the color of time. He was in the very first issue of *Passaic Review*, along with Allen Ginsberg; in *International Poetry Review, Oleander Review, Quarterday*, and many other journals. Ron's eBooks include *You are once again the stranger, Poems for the Narrow,* and *Stories of Love and Hate,* available at Amazon, BN, iTunes, and elsewhere. He lives with his beautiful sociologist wife in the New Jersey suburbs, where he can visit William Carlos Williams' grave anytime he likes.

Glenn A. Bruce

MFA, was associate fiction editor for The *Lindenwood Review*. He has published eight novels and two collections of short stories. He wrote *Kickboxer*, and episodes of

Walker: Texas Ranger and *Baywatch*. His stories, poems, and essays have been published internationally. He won *About That's* "Down and Dirty" short story contest and is a two-time finalist in the *Defenstrationism* annual contest. He teaches Screenwriting at Appalachian State University. Find his website at www.glennabruce.com.

Steve Carter

is a writer and jazz guitarist. He taught music and English at Berklee College of Music. His first book of poems, *Intermodulations*, was recently published by Maat Publishing (www.maatpublishing.net). His poetry has appeared in many magazines, including *Hanging Loose, Carolina Review, Stand,* and *Clackamas Literary Review.* His Writer's Journal can be found here at www.maatpublishing.net/steve/writers_journal. His music is available at www.frogstoryrecords.com.

Guilie Castillo Oriard

is a Mexican writer and dog rescuer living in Curaçao. She misses Mexican food and Mexican *amabilidad*, but the island's diversity and the laissez-faire attitude (and the beaches) are fair exchange. Her work has appeared online and in print. Her first book, *The Miracle of Small Things*, was published in August 2015 by Truth Serum Press. She blogs at http://guilie-castillo-oriard.blogspot.com and at http://lifeindogs.blogspot.com/.

Embe Charpentier

has been published in numerous literary magazines, including *Poydras Review, Indianola Review,* and *The Quotable*, and her first book *Beloved Dead*, is published by Kellan Books. Visit her website www.embecharpentier.com or follow her on twitter @embecharpentier.

Kersten Christianson

is a raven-watching, moon-gazing, high school English-teaching Alaskan. Currently she is pursuing her MFA in Creative Writing/Poetry through the University of Alaska Anchorage and will earn her degree in July 2016. Her recent work has appeared in *Cirque, Tidal Echoes, The Fredericksburg Literary & Art Review, We'Moon* and *On the Rusk.* Kersten co-edits the quarterly journal, *Alaska Women Speak.* She lives in Sitka, Alaska.

Martin Christmas

lives in Adelaide, South Australia; has an M.A. in Australian Cultural Studies; and is a performance poet, photographer and professional theatre director with one hundred productions under his belt. He was a mentored poet in 2012 and has been published in several Australian anthologies. He teaches presentation elements to young spoken word poets and has run community poetry workshops for established poets.

Jan Chronister

is a recently retired writing teacher and a former costume designer. She lives in the woods near Maple, Wisconsin with her husband and crabby cat. Her chapbook *Target Practice* was published in 2009 by Parallel Press (University of Wisconsin Libraries).

Jessica Clements

studied English at the University of Adelaide. You can read another of her stories in Pure Slush, volume 10, *Five.*

Paul B. Cohen

holds degrees from the University of Leeds, Vanderbilt University, and the University of Southern California. Based in England, his plays have been produced in Los Angeles, Miami, Orlando, and New York City. Recent short stories have appeared in *Poetica*, *Conclave*, *Gold Dust*, *Spelk* and *Prole*. 'Lecha Dodi' won first place in the 2014 Moment-Karma Foundation Short Fiction Awards and was published in *Moment* magazine. His website: https://paulbcohen.com.

Bruce Colbert

is a former journalist, and an actor and playwright in New York City. His plays have been performed Off-Broadway, and in Toronto. He is the author of four books.

Samuel Cole

lives in Woodbury, MN, where he finds work in special event management. He is a poet, flash fiction geek, and essayist enthusiast. His work has appeared in many literary journals. He is also a prize-winning card maker and scrapbooker.

Michael Coolen

is a composer, actor, performance artist, and writer. He has been published in *The Gold Man Review*, *Best Travel Stories*, *The Fable Online*, *Kalnya Language Press*, *Twisted Vine*, *Clementine Poetry Journal*, *Creative Writing Institute*, *Broken Plate Poetry Magazine*, and more. He is a published composer, whose works have been performed at Carnegie Hall, New England Conservatory of Music, Museum of Modern Art, and the Christie Gallery.

Gay Degani

has had three flash pieces nominated for Pushcart consideration and won the 11th Glass Woman Prize. Pure Slush Books published her collection, *Rattle of Want*, in 2015 and the second edition of her suspense novel, *What*

Came Before was published by Truth Serum Press in late 2016. She blogs at *Words in Place*.

Jon Dietrick

is Assistant Professor of English at Babson College, in Wellesley, Massachusetts. He mostly teaches and writes about drama. When he isn't doing that, Jon writes songs, short fiction, and short plays.

Kristina England

resides in Worcester, Massachusetts. Her writing has been published in several magazines, including *Gargoyle*, *Muddy River Poetry Review*, *New Verse News*, and *Silver Birch Press*. Her first set of published photos appeared at *Foliate Oak Literary Magazine* in April 2016.

Ruby Ewens

is originally from Adelaide and is a newly Melbourne-based writer and blogger. Her blog "Honest Bites" features her flash fiction. She also has poetry, fiction and non-fictions published by Midnight Sun Publishing and Hive Magazine.

Tom Fegan

was raised in his family's downtown Fort Worth Restaurant Burger & Shake. After college he spent several years in the steel industry and is presently contentedly divorced and works as a security professional. This gives him opportunity to pursue his writing career.

Linda Ferguson

has been published in numerous journals. She's won awards for her poetry, a Pushcart nomination for fiction and the Perceptions Magazine award for nonfiction. She's also the author of a poetry chapbook, *Baila Conmigo*, and teaches creative writing classes for adults and children. Find more about Linda here: www.bylindaferguson.blogspot.com.

Thomas Fucaloro

is the author of two books of poetry published by Three Rooms Press, most recently *It Starts from the Belly and Blooms*, which received rave reviews. The winner of a performance grant from the Staten Island Council of the Arts and the NYC Department of Cultural Affairs, he has been on three national slam teams. He holds an MFA in creative writing from the New School and is a cofounding editor of Great Weather for Media and NYSAI press. He is a writing coordinator at the Harlem Children's Zone and lives in Staten Island.

Brad Garber

has degrees in biology, chemistry and law. He writes, paints, draws, photographs, hunts for mushrooms and snakes, and runs around naked in the Great Northwest. Since 1991, he has published poetry, essays and weird stuff in such publications as *Edge Literary Journal, Pure Slush, Clementine Poetry Journal, Sugar Mule, Barrow Street, Aji Magazine* and other quality publications. He is a 2013 Pushcart Prize nominee.

Walter Giersbach

bounces between writing genres, from mystery to humor, speculative fiction to romance with a little non-fiction thrown in for good measure. His work has appeared in print and online in over two dozen publications. Two volumes of short stories, *Cruising the Green of Second Avenue*, are available at Barnes & Noble, Amazon and other online booksellers. He's also bounced from Fortune 500 firms to university posts, and from homes in eight states to a couple of Asian countries.

Chris Gillies

is a technical writer, journalist and sometime copywriter based in Newtown New South Wales. He has work published in the US, Australia and the UK and specializes in farming. He grew up on the coast, lives in the city, loves coffee, the gym, dogs, cats and enjoys writing short stories in his spare time. You can find out more about him at www.chrisgillies.com.

Kate Hall

lectures in Literary Studies at Deakin University, Geelong, Australia. She writes fiction and non-fiction, with recent work appearing in *Overland*, *The Grapple Annual no. 1* and *New Community*.

Cynthia Hoffman

is the daughter of Jewish refugees and draws upon the rich memories of her early childhood years among the immigrant communities of L.A.'s Boyle Heights. Happily retired, she participates in a writing group in Orinda, California where she first shared her writing and found her voice. She writes poetry and prose, fiction and creative non-fiction, and is a recent winner of the Western States Poetry Contest. Whatever wild spark ignites her imagination – nature's phenomena or becoming a vessel for characters she's never known – she writes until her eyes burn to find out what happens next.

Mark Hudson

lives in Evanston, Illinois, and he writes on a ninety-degree summer day. He just bought some lemonade from some kids, and he thinks they spit in his lemonade. Either he is paranoid, or the world really is out to get him. Nonetheless, he is having a great summer besides his ornery side. But what do you expect in ninety degree weather? A saint? His best work comes out of self-reflection when he makes mistakes, feels like a fool, then laughs it all off just to do it again. Right about now, he wishes he was swimming!

A.J. Huffman

has had poetry, fiction, haiku, and photography appear in hundreds of national and international journals, including *Labletter*, *The James Dickey Review*, and *Offerta Speciale*, in which her work appeared in both English and Italian translation. She is also the founding editor of Kind of a Hurricane Press: www.kindofahurricanepress.com.

Abha Iyengar

is an award winning, internationally published poet, author, editor, translator (Hindi to English), and a British Council certified creative writing mentor. She was a finalist in the FlashMob 2013 Flash Fiction contest. Her flash fiction has appeared in *The Indo-Australian Anthology of Short Fiction*. Her published works are *Yearnings*, *Flash Bites*, *Shrayan*, *Many Fish to Fry* and *The Gourd Seller and Other Stories*. Find her website at www.abhaiyengar.com and her blog at www.abhaencounter.blogspot.in.

Joanne Jagoda

retired in 2009, and it took one inspiring writing workshop to launch her on her writing journey. Joanne's short stories, poetry and nonfiction appear online and in print anthologies including *Pure Slush*, *Gemini*, and *Persimmon Tree Magazine*. In 2015, she was nominated for a Pushcart Prize. Joanne enjoys Zumba, traveling and hanging with her five grandchildren. Her blog, *My Detour*, chronicles her nine-month treatment for breast cancer.

Katie Rendon Kahn

lives on the Gulf Coast of Florida. Her poems have appeared in *Blackwater Review, Broken Publications, Diverse Voices Quarterly, The Barefoot Review, Rising Phoenix Press, Poetry Breakfast, Chaotic Review, Multiracial Media*, and various blogs. Kahn won the *Blackwater Review*'s Editor's Prize in 2012 and 2014. She co-wrote a children's book series with her 11-year-old daughter that you can find at worldadventuresseries.com.

S. L. Kerns

has southern roots in Kentucky, but has branched out to a life in Asia. After six years in Bangkok, he moved to Japan, where he teaches English. When his face isn't in a book, he is training for bodybuilding competitions. Find his work in *Flash Fiction Magazine, Silver Birch Press, Eastlit, Kill Those Damn Cats, Out of the Cave, 47-16* and more. Follow him here: www.slkerns.wordpress.com.

Michael Koenig (Falling Pieces of Skylab)

is a writer and editor from Oakland, California whose stories have appeared in recent issues of *The MacGuffin, Harpur Palate, Kentucky Review, Drunk Monkeys, Literary Orphans, The Crime Factory, Hardboiled*, and the *Paterson Literary Review*. His work has been anthologized in *Awake! A Reader for the Sleepless* (Soft Skull Press) and *The Shamus Sampler 2*, an international detective fiction collection.

Michael Koenig (Rot)

is an emerging queer poet and creative writing major at the University of Adelaide. His work is mainly concerned with queer anxieties, the beauty of nature and housewives (real or otherwise). When he's not writing poetry he enjoys overanalyzing PJ Harvey records, vegan food, avoiding social media and gardening.

Laurie Kolp

serves as President of Texas Gulf Coast Writers and Treasurer for Beaumont Poetry Society, a chapter of the Poetry Society of Texas. She has a full-length collection *Upon the Blue Couch* (Winter Goose Publishing) and chapbook *Hello, it's Your Mother* (Finishing Line Press). Laurie's poetry has appeared in *Scissors & Spackle*, *Driftwood Press*, *concis*, *Prelude*, and more. Keep up with her on Twitter (@KolpLaurie) or at http://lauriekolp.com.

Len Kuntz

is a writer from Washington State, an editor at the online magazine *Literary Orphans*, and the author of *I'm Not Supposed to be Here and Neither are You* out now from *Unknown Press*. You can also find more of his work here: lenkuntz.blogspot.com.

Jenny Lapekas

is a part-time college professor in Pennsylvania. Her work has appeared on the website *Bitch Flicks*, in addition to *Broad!* magazine, *Jump Cut*, *Women's Reproductive Health*, *Avalon Literary Review*, *Muddy River Poetry Review*, and "re:Cycling," the official blog of the Society for Menstrual Cycle Research, as well as the technology anthology, *TECH-OLOGY: a nonfiction anthology about our digital lives*. She blogs about food, film and literature at https://lotusgurl.wordpress.com.

Cynthia Leslie-Bole

is a writing coach, editor and Amherst Writers and Artists Method group leader. Her first collection of poetry, *The Luminous In-Between* (2016, Azalea Arts Press), invites us to experience the radiance of one woman's evolution through marriage, motherhood, spiritual individuation, and kinship with nature. Cynthia's lyrical poetry celebrates our innate capacity to create, heal, and perceive what lies beyond the ordinary in 'the luminous in-between.' Find more of her work here at www.theluminousinbetween.blogspot.com and www.cynthialesliebole.com.

Poor Louisiana

is from Belcher, Louisiana but now resides in San Antonio, Texas. She began writing poetry at the young age of eight. Her work *Sunrise at Sunset* and *Dancing in the Rain* has been recently published in the *Texas Writers Journal*. In the near future, she has high hopes of becoming an author while gaining a degree in English.

Janet Malotky

lives a life submersed in language, by day as a speech / language pathologist, and in the evening as a poet. She is especially intrigued by the mysteries at the intersection of language, science, and the inner human experience.

Erica Gerald Mason

is an author, poet and blogger living in Georgia. Her book of poetry, *i am a telescope: science love poems* is available on Kindle and in paperback on Amazon. Find her blog and poetry at www.ericageraldmason.com.

Piet Nieuwland

worked in conservation management after training as a forester. His poems have been published in many places including *Landfall, Printout, Brief, We Society Poetry Anthology, Globe Tapes, Live Lines, Mattoid, Takahe, Snafu, Tongue In Your Ear, Poetry NZ, NZPSA Journal,* and *The Blue Note Review*. He is editor of *Fast Fibres*

Poetry 3 and a poetry reviewer for *Landfall Online Review*. Found out more at www.fastfibres.wordpress.com and http://teaokikokiko.tumblr.com/.

Edward O'Dwyer

is from Limerick, Ireland, where he lives. His poems have featured in journals and anthologies throughout the world, including *The Forward Book of Poetry 2015* (Faber & Faber). He was selected by Poetry Ireland for their Introductions Series (2010). He has been nominated for Pushcart and Forward Prizes, and shortlisted for a Hennessy Award, among others. His first collection is *The Rain on Cruise's Street* (Salmon Poetry, 2014).

Sara Petersen

lives on the seacoast of New Hampshire. Sara's educational and professional background is in literature and education (and once upon a time, theatre). She's written essays for *Brain, Child, Huffington Post, Bust, Neutrons Protons*, and *Bustle*. She blogs at http://sara-petersen.com, and is on Twitter and Instagram.

Tim Philippart

sold his business, retired to explore, to write and discovered he wasn't very retired at all. He ghost blogs, writes poetry, non-fiction and an occasional magazine piece. He loves writing and wishes he had not waited decades to pick up the pen. He sees baseball as a metaphor for… Oh, he's sorry, he keeps promising not to do that. Send emails to timphilippart@yahoo.com and visit www.imaginiscent.net.

Ben Pitts

is from Phoenix, Arizona. A High School English teacher by day and a renegade poet by night, he lives with his wife,

Brianne and daughter, Grace. His poetry has been featured on several websites and journals and most recently in *The Machinery* literary collection.

Martin Jon Porter

is a 34-year-old teacher who lives in Brunswick, Melbourne. He has had poetry published in *Positive Words*, *Idiom 23* as well as the international art and literature journal *ArtAscent*. He has just returned from a three month sojourn in Central and South America. He is a real person.

Matt Potter

is an Australian-born writer who keeps a part of his psyche in Berlin. Matt has been published in various places online, and you can find more of his work including details of his travel memoir *Hamburgers and Berliners and other courses in between* (Cervena Barva Press, 2015), his collections *Vestal Aversion* (Pure Slush Books, 2012) and *Based on True Stories* (Truth Serum Press, 2016), and his ESL teaching resources *all you need is … a whiteboard, a marker and this book Volumes 1 and 2* (Everytime Press, 2016), at his website http://mattcpotter.webs.com/.

MK Punky

is the best-selling author of many books, most recently *The Termite Squad* (Eggy Press). MK's essays, articles and poems have appeared everywhere from the New York Times to international literary journals, including Pure Slush 11.

Stephen V. Ramey

lives in beautiful New Castle, Pennsylvania, with his wife and two reformed feral cats. His work has appeared in many places, including *The Journal of Compressed Creative Arts*, *The Doctor T. J. Eckleburg Review*, and *Every Day*

Fiction. His collection of (very) short fictions, *Glass Animals* (Pure Slush Books), is available wherever fine books are e-sold. More at www.stephenvramey.com and on facebook and twitter (@svramey).

Martha Rand

is a writer and artist. Her fiction has been published in Pure Slush anthologies *obit*, and *barcode* as well as at the *Pure Slush* online site. Her work has been read at galleries in New Jersey and at KGB in New York City. Her artwork has been shown in juried shows in New York and New Jersey. Ms. Rand has been a Licensed Clinical Social Worker for over 20 years. ArtsHealer.com is her website.

Edward Reilly

was born in Adelaide, and holds an MA in Literary Studies and a PhD in Poetics. He has been active in Geelong's literary scene since the late 1970s and is the founding editor of *Azuria* (Geelong Writers). He is the author of several VCE English and Literature study guides for VATE and Insight, and published a memoir, *First Snow*, in 2004. His poetry and prose have been published in Australian journals and overseas.

Sally Reno

has been among the winners of National Public Radio's 3-Minute Fiction Contest, the *Dr. T. J. Eckleburg Review* Prosetry Contest, and she has been nominated for the Pushcart Prize. She lives in a vaporish grotto where she serves as Pythoness to *Blink Ink Print* and Haruspex for *Shining Mountains Press*.

Alex Robertson

was raised in Adelaide and spent his early working life around (country) South Australia and the Northern

Territory. He has been published, first in university student publications and more recently in print and online journals. Since his location to the Adelaide Plains he has been involved in writing groups and broadcasting organisations around the north-eastern suburbs of Adelaide and Gawler.

Ruth Sabath Rosenthal

is a New York poet, well-published in literary journals and poetry anthologies throughout the U.S. and internationally. In October 2006, her poem *on yet another birthday* was nominated for a Pushcart prize. Ruth has authored five books of poetry: *Facing Home* (a chapbook); *Facing Home and beyond; little, but by no means small; Food: Nature vs Nurture;* and *Gone, but Not Easily Forgotten.* Purchase these books from amazon.com. For more about Ruth, visit her website at www.newyorkcitypoet.com or her blog at www.poetrybyruthsabathrosenthal.com.

W. Jack Savage (cover art)

is a retired broadcaster and educator. He is the author of seven books including *Imagination: The Art of W. Jack Savage* (wjacksavage.com). To date, more than fifty of Jack's short stories and over eight hundred of his paintings and drawings have been published worldwide. Jack and his wife Kathy live in Monrovia, California.

Iris N. Schwartz

is a fiction writer, as well as a Pushcart-Prize-nominated poet. Most recently, her work has appeared in *Grabbing the Apple: An Anthology of Poems by New York Women Writers*; and in such journals as *The Gambler, Gravel, Jellyfish Review, MUSH/MUM Journal,* and *Siren.*

Beate Sigriddaughter

lives and writes in New Mexico, the Land of Enchantment, USA. Her work has received four Pushcart Prize nominations and won four poetry awards. She blogs at https://writinginawomansvoice.blogspot.com/ and you can also find her work at www.sigriddaughter.com.

J. J. Steinfeld

lives on Prince Edward Island, where he is patiently waiting for Godot's arrival and a phone call from Kafka. While waiting, he has published sixteen books, including *Disturbing Identities* (Stories, Ekstasis Editions), *Would You Hide Me?* (Stories, Gaspereau Press), *Misshapenness* (Poetry, Ekstasis Editions), *Identity Dreams and Memory Sounds* (Poetry, Ekstasis Editions), and *Madhouses in Heaven, Castles in Hell* (Stories, Ekstasis Editions).

Penn Stewart

lives and writes in Wichita Falls, Texas, where he teaches creative writing at Midwestern State University. He is the author of the novel *Fertile Ground* from Knox Robinson Publishing, and his most recent short fiction has appeared in *Corvus Review*, *Literary Orphans*, *Word Riot*, *Dogzplot*, *Union Station Magazine*, and elsewhere. You can learn more about Penn by visiting his website www.pennstewart.com.

Lisa Stice

received a BA in English literature from Mesa State College (now Colorado Mesa University) and an MFA in creative writing and literary arts from the University of Alaska Anchorage. She is a military wife who lives in North Carolina with her husband, daughter and dog. She is the author of a full-length poetry collection, *Uniform* (Aldrich Press, 2016). Find out more about her and her publications at lisastice.wordpress.com and facebook.com/LisaSticePoet.

Susan Tally

works in New York's Public School 163 as a literacy tutor. One of her favorite subjects to write about is her cat Zoey. Her poems have appeared in *Birds Piled Loosely* (Issues One and Five), *Clementine Poetry Journal* (Volume 1), and *Kind of Hurricane Press* (Anthology 3, 4).

Devin Taylor

studies English and Creative Writing at Washington College in Chestertown, Maryland. He reads poetry at open mic-nights all over the Washington DC area, sometimes under the pseudonym 'Chuck E. Cheese'. He has been published in *The Lake* (UK), *The Poeming Pigeon*, *In Between Hangovers*, *Five 2 One*, *MUSH/MUM*, *Gargoyle*, and *Silicon Heart Zine*. He plays electric kazoo and eats his fruit and vegetables.

Michael Webb

is a pharmacist by profession, a writer by avocation, and a lover of punctuation. You can find his other writings online at michaelwebb.us.

Mercedes Webb-Pullman

gained an MA in Creative Writing from Victoria University, Wellington, in 2011. Her poems and short stories have appeared online and in print, including *Turbine*, *4th Floor*, *Swamp*, *Reconfigurations*, *The Electronic Bridge*, *Otoliths*, *Connotations*, *The Red Room*, *Typewriter*, *Cliterature*, and *Pure Slush* among others, and in her books. She lives on the Kapiti Coast, New Zealand.

Judy Williams

lives and writes in Belfast, ME, and is recently retired from her position as Writing Center Director and instructor of

English at Unity College. She has had poems and short stories published in *Cardinal Flower Journal: Creative Reflections of Northern New England, Off the Coast, Out of the Cradle, Stolen Island Review,* and *Crosscut Literary Magazine.* She has reviewed books and published freelance articles for various print media.

Allan J. Wills

lives in rural Western Australia where he works as an entomologist during the day, helps his Japanese-born wife raise his second batch of children, and writes small scenes from life during his spare time at night.

Alicja Zapalska

is a Polish-American writer currently living in Austin, Texas. She has been published in *Jet Fuel Review, Winter Tangerine Review,* and *The Postscript Journal.*

Other books from Pure Slush

Visit the Pure Slush Store:
http://pureslush.webs.com/store.htm

Feast!
ISBN: 978-1-925101-62-1

Five
ISBN: 978-1-925101-71-3

tall...ish
ISBN: 978-1-925101-80-5

Rattle of Want
ISBN: 978-1-925101-67-6

The Vixen Scream
ISBN: 978-1-925101-11-9

Many Fish to Fry
ISBN: 978-1-925101-59-1

www.ingramcontent.com/pod-product-compliance
Lightning Source LLC
Chambersburg PA
CBHW052142170626
46812CB00004B/1548